Stockholm Diaries, Caroline

A Destination Romance

by

REBECCA HUNTER

ACKNOWLEDGMENTS

There are many people who have helped make this book possible. First, I'd like to thank my list of Beta readers/editors/problem-finders, who tolerated this book in its less-than-finished state: Julia Victorine, Laura Burtness, Micki Gray and Wendi Wakefield. Your insights have helped shape the story on all levels. In this category, I'd like to especially thank my sister, Leah, Beta-reader extraordinaire and general cheerleader for all my writing projects. Thanks for happily reading everything I've ever written, including the pieces that never should have left my computer.

I'd also like to thank my writing partner, K.D. Hazzard, for her support and humor and for walking me through everything from plot crisis to momentum crisis. And to all the members of the San Francisco Area chapter of Romance Writers of American who have shared their expertise, tips and insights, I thank you for making this project as a whole possible.

And last, I'd like to thank my husband, sometimes hockey player and always at the heart of my own Stockholm Diaries adventures. Thank you for your patience and support as I've worked to turn a hobby into something more.

1
A wooden spoon has many uses

Everyone knows that a woman shouldn't be out walking alone in the middle of the night. Especially if she's from Detroit, which I was.

Yet where did I find myself? Alone, in the middle of Stockholm somewhere around 4:00 am, and not for the first time this week. But it was light out. At least that was my reasoning when I stuffed my pepper spray into my pocket before closing the apartment door behind me.

It wasn't just the canopy of trees overhead or the muted sound that pulled me out this early, onto the winding paths of Vasaparken. Everything about the light in Stockholm was different. A gentle mist had settled low along the steep hills of the city park, veiling the tops of the impossibly tall pine trees that lined the sidewalk.

I took the lens cap off my camera and pointed it up at the trees, looking through the viewfinder. For the last few years now, I had developed a preference for the starkness of black and white, the depth and texture that it could capture, but a week in Stockholm had changed that. It was the fullness, the clear, deep blue sky and the endless layers of greens in the trees that I looked for at all hours of the day. Since I had arrived, the sun seemed to never completely disappear, only fading into a slow twilight and then inching back up again, just barely having sunk below the horizon. It was as if I had come to some sort of mystical world, one I had been given all to myself in these early mornings.

Though clearly this was a mystical world without the dangers of wandering alone at night. How else could I explain my obvious disregard for the rule that had been drilled into my mind since I was a child: don't go out alone at night, not even in a clean European city that felt more storybook than real.

Especially not if the person in question had a rather traditional Mexican father…which I did. Whether or not I agreed with this rule, it was hard to forget completely. But the jet lag that had stubbornly followed since my recent arrival from Michigan meant that I found myself waking up at odd hours of the night anyway. And this was what I had traveled across the Atlantic for, wasn't it? Adventure, photography, and freedom.

I looked through my photos, studying each one on the tiny screen, until I scrolled too far. Instead of this mystical land, Brad was staring back at me. I had taken one last photo of him before I left, and clearly he hadn't been happy about it. Or, rather, he hadn't been happy with me. He had tried all methods of persuasion to get me to stay. After all, persuasion was what he was good at.

I let out a sigh of frustration. I was *not* going to waste my time in Stockholm on Brad.

My thoughts were interrupted by rowdy shouts from a group of men passing by. I hadn't noticed them coming up the park path, and now they were too close to completely avoid. They all looked larger than average, though Sweden seemed to be full of this size of guy. I put my hand on the pepper spray in my pocket and looked up at the group.

"Vill du komma hem med mig?" called a guy in a baseball hat. This earned a few chuckles from the group.

Shit. I had no idea what that meant, but by the tone, I could tell it wasn't anything good. My heart was pumping the message, *danger, danger,* loud in my ears. The best thing to do was to stay quiet and see what happened. But while the rest of the group continued to walk on, Baseball Cap stopped not far from me, clearly waiting for his answer.

Was this just going to pass, or was he serious? I took a shaky breath, clutching my pepper spray tighter. He didn't move. Then, from out of the crowd, another guy came forward—a big, blond, living stereotype of a Nordic Viking. Husky shoulders. Ripped muscles peeking out from the sleeves of his t-shirt. I stared as he slowly approached, his eyes fixed on Baseball Cap, and when he spoke, his voice was quiet but firm.

"*Låt henne va'.*"

Whatever Viking Guy had said had an effect. Baseball Cap turned to look at Viking Guy. He glanced one more time at me and then turned away to join the group again.

Viking Guy turned and faced me for the first time. His shaggy blond hair fell over deep blue eyes, almost hiding them, but when he looked right at me, they were bright and clear. Whoa. My heart pounded harder, though it was no longer out of fear. No, this guy's look was entirely different from Baseball Cap's. Despite the fact that the park at night was just about the least appropriate place to size up a man, a very large one, in fact, I was doing just that...before I caught myself. My cheeks flushed, and I gave him a little smile I hoped would show gratitude. His eyes still fixed on mine, he gave me a hint of a smile that made my heart jump again. Then Viking Guy took a visible breath and nodded, turning away. The group walked down the path and across the street, toward the subway station.

I closed my eyes and took a couple more shaky breaths. I had pepper spray. I would have used it if Baseball Cap had come closer.

Something rustled behind me, and I whipped around, but it was just a leaf scraping the sidewalk. I looked down at my camera. The magic of my morning was long gone. The mist was beginning to dissolve from Vasaparken's hills, and the first cars sped down

Odengatan. And I was a little shaken up. Time to go back.

I crossed the empty street and walked up to a formal-looking stone building, one of many, old and tightly packed into the long block. Looking up, I counted the windows until I came to a balcony on the third floor. My balcony—for this month, at least. I punched in the building code and walked through the entry, towards the stairs. My body was begging to give in to sleep. Just a few more minutes, and I'd be in bed.

I gazed up the marble steps that spiraled along the rounded walls of the stairwell and disappeared. Waaaay too many stairs. I glanced over at the tiny elevator next to me and frowned. As a rule, I had taken the steps all week, half-afraid of shutting myself into the tiny box, made for "*max. 2 personer*"—even I could read that much Swedish. The elevator looked as old as the building itself, but today, my weary legs got the better of me.

I pulled on the wooden door and slid open the metal gate just beyond it. The door closed behind me, and I pushed my floor number and crossed my fingers. Nothing happened. I pushed it again. Nothing. I groaned. It wasn't the first time this week that I had spent a good while trying to figure out how basic things worked here—the coffee pot, the shower handle and even the light switch, for God's sake. I fought twinges of frustration as I jiggled the metal gate and pushed the button one more time. The elevator still didn't move.

I gritted my teeth and resigned myself to the stairs. But as I was about to grab the handle of the heavy wooden door, it was yanked out of reach. Before I could step out, a bulk of a man pushed his way in. The "*max 2 personer*" sign clearly didn't have a guy like this in mind, but he didn't seem to care. I shrank back into the corner of the elevator, looking for a little more space.

He managed to close the gate with a satisfying click, and the elevator jolted to life on the first try. I flattened myself against the back of the wooden, closet-like space, the view directly in front of me blocked by the broad shoulders that pulled at the seams of this man's t-shirt. Without thinking, my gaze lingered on these shoulders and the thick, muscular arms that almost brushed against me. Something made me look away, my heart pounding. I took a deep breath, and the smell of beer and stale cigarettes assaulted me. *Ugh*. At first the man seemed not to notice my presence, but then he muttered something in Swedish—to me, I assumed, since no one else was there.

The elevator creaked and rattled as it made its way up until, with a ding, the little carriage came to a sudden stop at my floor. How I would squeeze myself around this hulk of a man? And how did he know my floor? But as I considered these questions, he opened the gate and stepped out, letting the door close unceremoniously onto me. Quickly, I pushed it open again and stepped out onto the landing of the third floor. The staircase curled around to my right, and to my left, there was the dark landing for the building's two third-floor apartments.

The man walked up to the door opposite mine and began fumbling with his keys. I took a step towards my door and then stopped, staring unabashedly as I got a better look at the guy. Was it…Viking Guy from the park? Or was it another one of his Nordic god look-alikes? I wasn't sure, but the thought of seeing Viking Guy again made my heart jump. I had never seen my neighbor, but on my first night, I had heard him through the walls. And what I had heard hadn't made me interested in knocking on the door to introduce myself.

I continued to stare at him until the clatter of his keys on the ground startled me out of my thoughts. I turned away, thinking he had caught me staring, but he still didn't seem to notice me at all. As he bent down to pick them up, I reached into my own pockets. My keys weren't there.

"Shit. Not again," I groaned.

The words slipped out of my mouth before I could stop them. The man turned around and looked at me as if he were seeing me for the first time. It *was* Viking Guy—I was sure of it—and now his clear blue eyes were staring at me again. I thought I saw a glimmer of recognition.

"*Du,*" he said under his breath. Then he asked, "Are you American?"

His eyes were even more intense up close.

Something about their color drew me in. They were not unlike the colors I had tried to capture with my camera only minutes before. In another light, I might not have noticed them, further hidden behind a few days of stubble and a bruise on his cheek that I hadn't seen earlier. But he looked at me again in the same way he had in the park, a way that made me suddenly feel his entire presence. And my own. And just for a moment, I forgot everything else.

I blinked. He had asked me a question. What was it? About being American.

"Yes, I am," I said.

"That's why you didn't say anything," he said softly.

I assumed he was talking about the park, about why I didn't respond to Baseball Cap's provocation. But I didn't want to think about Baseball Cap right now.

Instead, I nodded. "And I forgot my keys again."

While the self-locking door on this flat was supposed to be a helpful safety feature, there were clearly downsides to the set-up. Especially since it was too early to wake up Veronica for the spare key. Luckily, my friend had shown me the trick to breaking in if this ever happened. The door handles were different from the knobs I was used to in my Michigan apartment. These were three-inch rods that opened when pulled down. If the top bolt lock wasn't fastened, a slim arm could slip through the mail slot and reach for the handle. If that arm was long enough. It was time to find out.

Determined to focus on the dilemma at hand and not the formidable man only a few feet away from me, I knelt down next to the door and shimmied my forearm through the mail slot. It barely fit, and the metal scraped at my skin. Suddenly, half way into the process of breaking in, I felt the man's gaze heavy on me. This strange man was watching me with interest. A large man with intense blue eyes. I turned back to him, and he seemed to read my hesitancy.

"Don't worry. There's no way I could fit my arm through there," he said with a chuckle. We both looked down at his long, muscular forearms, easily twice the size of mine. "I just want to see if you can do this."

I stretched my arm out as flat as possible, working it slowly through the slot. Finally, my elbow crossed through to the inside, and I bent my arm up, reaching around. Nothing but the wooden door. After a few minutes of groping, I gave up. My arm wasn't long enough.

Slowly, I dragged my arm out and sighed. Then I looked up at Viking Guy. He was still watching me from only a few feet away with a look I couldn't quite read. Amusement and something else.

"Wait here," he said, as if I had any other choice.

This time, his key found the keyhole, and the door to his apartment swung open. I watched as he retreated down an empty hall. Every Swede I had met so far had spoken English with a sophisticated-sounding British accent, the Swedish school standard, apparently, but this guy's English was clearly American and sounded comfortable. He must have some connection there, I thought, judging from his reaction to my accent. But before I had a chance to think more about it, he reappeared with a long, wooden spoon in his hand.

"Try this. You can hook the handle with it," he said, handing the spoon to me. "Someone might as well get use out of it."

The corner of his mouth twitched up into a little smile, and I couldn't help but smile back. So this guy had a sense of humor.

I knelt back down and wedged my arm through the opening again, spoon in hand, until my elbow passed through to the other side of the mail slot. So far, so good. The handle of the spoon should be long enough if I could get the angle right. I waved it around, but it just swished and banged on the wooden door. *Closer*. I swung the spoon a little harder, but I hit the handle sooner than I had expected. With a clang, the spoon fell out of my hand.

"Shit," I muttered.

He raised his eyebrows. "I'll be back," he said and disappeared down his hall again.

He returned with a wooden spatula this time.

"It's your last chance," he said, holding it just out of reach. "My kitchen is pretty bare." Then he handed it over. His smile was a little wider this time.

I took the spatula with my free hand and fed it

through the slot, grabbing it with my other hand. That hand was the only part of my body that was going to enter my apartment this morning if I didn't get it right. This time, I held on tighter, and after a few more swings at the handle, I felt the spatula connect. I pulled down slowly until the latch clicked. The door glided open, taking my arm with it in a decidedly ungraceful pull. *Voila.*

"Impressive," he said. He moved closer to lift the metal flap as I extracted my arm from the narrow slot. It was a slow and slightly painful process, but, finally, I was free.

"Thanks," I said. I handed him the spatula and rubbed the raw scrapes down my arm. He released the metal slot and we both stood up. I was close enough to feel the warmth of his body next to mine, but I didn't step away, and neither did he. We were so standing so close. This was probably closer than a strange man should be in the earlier hours of the morning, but nothing about this situation felt threatening. In fact, it was starting to feel like something completely different.

I took another long drink of him and tried to steady my breath. The shoulders I had noticed in the elevator looked even broader from this angle, and his biceps flexed against the sleeves of his t-shirt. The view felt so…intimate. I bit my lip and continued looking up. Cut jaw underneath that scruff, full lips, and those sky-blue eyes.

But he wasn't looking at my face. I followed his

gaze down to the scratches on my arm. My heart thumped in my throat as he lifted his hand slowly toward the red marks by my elbow, and the pull between us grew stronger. And stronger. Finally, he touched my skin. A spark of hot desire simmered through me, strong and unexpected. I drew in a sharp breath, and he stepped back immediately.

Whoa. What had just happened between us?

Viking Guy was quickly retreating.

"Let me get your spoon," I said.

"Sorry," he mumbled at the same time, not looking at me anymore.

He turned back to his apartment and slammed the door before I had a chance to turn around.

2
"He slammed the door in your face?"

"So he stares at you in the park, helps you break in, touches your arm in a dark hallway and then slams the door in your face?" repeated Veronica, brushing the crumbs off her hand. "Sounds like a winner to me."

"I think he was a little drunk," I added as I took another bite of the gigantic cinnamon roll on the plate in front of me. "He smelled like beer and cigarettes."

"Mmm—even better."

So why had I gone back over those last moments in the hallway so many times? His gaze had been intense, curious, and his hand on my skin…I tried to stop myself before that thought went any further, but it was too late. Once again, I was replaying the moment he touched me, and my heart jumped and fluttered. Okay, he was officially hot, and based on all the other details I had just shared with Veronica, that probably wasn't a good thing.

The tiny café was mostly empty now. One lone man had his computer open, settled in for a longer haul—work, the look on his face suggested. All the other patrons had finished their coffee and pastries and then left, presumably not wanting to waste one of Stockholm's truly warm days indoors.

But Veronica and I made no move to get up, despite the fact that our second round of cinnamon rolls was almost gone. It felt so good to sit here with her. The two of us looked enough alike to be sisters around here, with our long, wavy brown hair and skin a few shades darker than anyone I had seen around this part of Stockholm. But somehow, despite the ten years that had passed since we had seen each other, Veronica had managed to keep the spark of optimism that I hadn't felt in myself for a long time.

"Well, I guess you should be happy. You got more out of him than anyone else in the building has," said Veronica. "He never even looks my way when I pass him on the stairs. Even when I've said hello, he just grunts and nods."

"Yeah, he grunted at me, too. But you don't know who he is?"

"He moved in not long before you arrived. And this is Sweden—people don't make friends with their neighbors. In fact, they avoid it," said Veronica with a laugh. "Something about respecting each other's privacy. Filip warned me against trying to talk to people in the halls when I first got here, but I still can't help it. You can take the girl out of Mexico…"

I snickered.

"It doesn't matter," I said, taking the last bite of my

cinnamon roll. "What I really need to be thinking about is life stuff, like how I'm going to fund my trip around the world. I spent most of my money on the plane ticket."

"How much does the ex-patriot interview job pay?"

"Not much at first, though if we can get a good readership, they'll pay more. There are three others working on this series, all on different continents. I need to come up with one article every two weeks, max two per country, through the summer. I'll have some spare time here, but after two articles in Sweden, I have to move on. Which gives me about a month total to figure out some other income sources. I have some savings, but not much."

"How about portraits? Baby portraits, maybe? Who's that woman—Anne Geddes? She must make heaps off of them. And people love their babies here in Sweden."

"Ugh." I sighed. Baby portraits were exactly what I was trying to put behind me. Though I was grateful for the job—many of my college friends had long given up any hope of making a living in photography by now—I found the mall studio where I had worked for the last six years depressing. I had left to get away from that kind of thing.

"No," I added decisively. "No more baby portraits. I want something real, something outside the studio. I really don't care what it is. I'm just tired of cleaning baby spit-up off the props. If that's what I wanted, I might as well have stayed in Michigan with Brad."

"No, you definitely should *not* have stayed with Brad, *Carolita*," said Veronica and shook her head vigorously. That got a laugh from me.

I agreed with Veronica, or at least I had when I bought my ticket a few months ago. Brad and I had actually planned to travel together "after I finish law school and get established," he had said when we moved in together. Now I wasn't sure he had ever intended to follow through on that promise. Did he say it just to get me to stay? He was always so rational, and his reasons made so much sense at the time, but over the years I had begun to suspect that his smooth demeanor was a calculated method for getting his way.

"Brad was nice, wasn't he?" I asked, almost to myself.

But Veronica's thoughts went in a different direction, and she waved her hand dismissively at my question. "Nice is something you want in your dentist, not the man you're having sex with every day."

I stifled a laugh with my hand.

"Did I say that too loudly?" she whispered.

I looked over at the man in the corner, who was clearly not paying attention to his laptop anymore.

"Yep, you did," I chuckled.

Veronica shook her head. "I'm always the loud one. Even after five years in Sweden, I still haven't learned to keep my voice down."

Veronica smoothed her dress and drank down the

last of her coffee. Then, in her best business voice, she said, "Now, back to planning your career."

"Planning is what usually gets me in trouble," I said with a sigh. "If I think too much, I end up making the safe decisions, not the decisions that make me happy."

"That's what I'm here for." Veronica's eyes were sparkling. She was clearly enjoying this.

"You already found me a place to stay in your building," I said. "You don't have to find me a job, too. Though something tells me you're going to try anyway." I reached across the table and squeezed my friend's hand. "I've missed you, Veronica."

"I've missed you, too. That's why I have to help you find a way to make money here," she said, her smile growing wider. "Maybe you'll stay longer."

"But my best connections are for travel publications, which means... well, travel. If this series gets some traction, I'll be able to pitch more ideas to this magazine and others. I'll get my foot in the door. I just need to eat in the meantime."

"There must be money somewhere else," said Veronica resting her chin on her hands. "How about sports? The hockey world championships are at The Globe in Stockholm starting next week—Filip bought tickets. I'm sure sports photography pays a lot, right?"

I raised my eyebrows and leaned back in my chair. "I guess so."

Sports photography probably did pay more if I

could get the right kind of shots. True, I hadn't shot a hockey game since college, but there must be something in common between the candid portraits I prided myself on and the action that surfaced on a hockey rink. And if there wasn't? I could come up with something.

"Hmm..." Veronica strummed her fingers on the table. "Filip knows someone who could probably get you a press pass," she said and then gave me a mischievous smile. "And this guy is single, too."

3
The social equivalent of slamming the door in my face

I turned the key—the one I had found waiting for me on the hall table, just out of reach when I had wielded the long spoon the morning before—and let myself back into the apartment. Even after a week of staying in this place, it was hard not to feel like I was invading someone else's life each time I walked in.

The couple that owned the apartment had left everything, large and small, when they took off for Brazil. Gustavsson was their name, Tommy and Annika Gustavsson, some sort of reference or joke in Swedish, I had gathered, judging from the way people who didn't know them chuckled at their names. Veronica had made the arrangements for me, so I had never met the couple in person, yet I had a strangely intimate knowledge of their everyday life.

They drank espresso rather than coffee. Veronica had to show me how to work the strange metal contraption that went on the stove instead of plugging into the wall. And they liked to travel, judging from the row of guides on their shelves. There were shelves of other books with indecipherable titles, some with small print and serious-looking covers and others in mass-market paperback. Definitely a reader in the family. The rooms were white, clutter-free and sparsely decorated with low, geometric furniture that was surprisingly comfortable. Tasteful but more like something out of a magazine than anything I'd seen in real homes before.

But it was the photographs that connected me to the phantom couple I was living with. While only a few abstract paintings hung on the living room and bedroom walls, the space behind the breakfast nook was covered with an eclectic mishmash of photos, all framed in black and artfully fit together into an intricate puzzle. The photos created a kind of travelogue of the couple's adventures together: Annika on top of a rocky cliff, long blond hair blowing behind her. Layers of white buildings rose up behind her in the distance on one side, water in Mediterranean blue on the other. In the photo below, Tommy was standing on the side of a busy city road somewhere in Asia, listening attentively to whatever the rickshaw driver was telling him.

There was just one photo of the two of them, standing in front of the Coliseum in Rome. The picture was not particularly well framed, their bodies cut off at the knees and the Coliseum at an odd angle, but I understood immediately why they had hung the photo up anyway. What it captured was probably a mistake. The photo seemed to be taken right before they were ready. Tommy was pushing the hair out of Annika's eyes as she laughed in a last-minute attempt to fix their pose. But instead of the usual smiling couple in front of a landmark, this photo captured a more intimate gesture that told of a different kind of happiness—not just happy to be in Rome but truly happy together.

Was it possible to know someone through photographs alone? At the very least, they hold a part of the people they capture, I thought as I sat down at Tommy and Annika's kitchen table. It's why I had brought a tiny photo collection of my own on this trip, now set up underneath the window in the bedroom. The photographs were pieces of the people I loved, pieces I wanted to hang onto.

But today was beautiful and warm, not a day to spend inside, looking at photos of a happy couple. And I had work to do. There were a few cafes along the park, potential spots to photograph my first subject: Veronica. And despite my procrastination, I wasn't worried. Veronica had always looked both lively and relaxed in pictures, with her easy smile even when caught off guard. I had finished most of the interview that morning, and when the editor mailed to ask if my first article was ready, I had said yes. This evening I'd pull it all together and send it out. Then, if I still had the energy, I could look into getting a press pass for the hockey tournament.

I grabbed what I had come back upstairs for: my laptop and camera. Then, double-checking for my keys this time, I opened up the door.

In front of me, only a few feet away, stood Viking Guy. He didn't turn around but just continued to unlock the door.

"Hi," I said, my voice echoing in the dark hallway.

"Hey." He nodded over his shoulder and then started to walk in. Was this what Veronica had referred to earlier—Swedish neighborly unfriendliness?

"Wait," I called just before he shut his door. "I still have your spoon."

I reached back onto the hall table and grabbed it. Then I walked over to his door, holding it out, as if offering proof. He stopped. After a long pause, he finally turned around. I drew in my breath a little louder than what was probably polite. He was bigger than I remembered, still unshaven but now with an angry red cut above his eye, patched together with a few surgical strips. I tried to keep the surprise off my face, though, judging from his look, I wasn't completely successful.

"Your spoon?" I said quietly, offering it again.

Finally, reluctantly, it seemed, he met my eyes. And when he did, I saw a fierceness in them that ran through me. I must have reacted, because he closed his eyes, and when he opened them, the look was gone. I opened my mouth to speak again, but nothing came out.

"Haven't missed it," he answered with a half-smile, taking the spoon from me. But as he grabbed it, his large hand brushed across mine, sending a jolt through me—the same crackle of attraction I had felt the other day. He seemed to feel it too, and his hand jerked back.

"Thanks," he muttered.

"I'm Caroline, by the way," I said.

He nodded and said, "Niklas," just before closing the door.

I remained there for a moment, my face only inches from the thick wood, trying to figure out if this guy had just slammed the door in my face again. He did, I decided as I turned back toward the stairwell. It was another good reason why I shouldn't waste my time thinking about him, in addition to the reason that had occurred to me the minute he had turned around: Why would a grown man, especially one as intent on avoiding other people as he seemed to be, have a cut over his eye? He looked like he had been in a fight. I couldn't help thinking that with his size, the other guy must look even worse. The image of him in the elevator—before the stench of beer and cigarettes took over, that is—came to me without warning: the broad thick shoulders, the long, tightly muscled arms. Something about the base physicality of those arms had made me avert my gaze, despite the fact that no one could see me staring. Now, my breath quickened again.

Enough. Judging by his abrupt exit, he certainly wasn't sitting at home thinking about me.

Even in the short time I had spent gathering my things from the apartment, the day had heated up, making the walk up Odengatan positively hot, with the shaded park across the street offering little relief. In fact, it was the first time the weather had approached anything near hot since I had arrived in Stockholm. Veronica had assured me earlier that warm summer weather was the exception, not the rule here.

"You're coming to a country where the sun barely rises for months. There are places up north where the snow hasn't completely melted yet."

I wasn't sure if this was fact or exaggeration, though by Veronica's tone I was inclined to believe the latter.

Odengatan stretched out in front of me. I gazed up at a tall yellow apartment building, sandwiched together against other similar structures along the street, all six stories high with dark metal roofs and various lookouts, all made of hundred-year-old stone and plaster. In Detroit, most things this old would be missing half its windows and be surrounded by empty lots, I thought with a wry smile. But here, people actually seemed to be living in these places. Even me, in fact.

I walked slowly down the street, peering in dark entranceways and down basement staircases. I peeked into the neighborhood "favorites" that Veronica had listed in my ex-patriot interview: The home-style restaurant hidden away on the side street around the corner that served Swedish pancakes and meatballs. The Italian kitchen shop at the end of the street, where I saw in the little display window the espresso maker Tommy and Annika had in their kitchen.

Finally, I found what I was looking for: the bakery.

I couldn't miss the smell of bread and cinnamon that wafted out onto the sidewalk. The glass windows that lined the front of the café were folded open, and inside the air was cooler. Perfect.

I ordered a coffee and stared at the cinnamon rolls that were piled high onto a glass cake platter. One more wouldn't hurt, not with all the walking I was doing…right? I found myself a seat that faced the park across the street and opened up my laptop.

It only took a minute or two of searching to find out what I should have guessed: Getting press passes for international hockey tournaments required a great deal of documentation about who I would be freelancing for, and, worse, the application deadline passed back in January. I leaned back in my chair and sighed. What were my options? Sneak in?

But the idea of shooting the hockey games had planted itself into me, and I wasn't ready to give up so easily. In fact, the more I thought about the idea, the more I was intrigued. I actually did have some experience in sports photography, even if it was many years ago. Back at the University of Michigan, I had worked for *The Michigan Daily*, basically doing any kind of photography the college newspaper needed. I never had much interest in hockey assignments. With a Mexican father and Texan mother, the family generally balked at the idea of going out into the cold voluntarily. Needless to say, hockey, along with other sports that required extra layers, was looked upon with skepticism by the Mendoza family.

Still, the photo that had received the most attention at the *Michigan Daily* was, in fact, one of my shots from the Big Ten hockey finals in Detroit. I had saved it in my personal portfolio, not because of the award I had won for it but because I had managed to capture the emotion of the game and the crowd around me in one, fixed moment.

I scrolled through my folders and found it. The game was University of Michigan versus Michigan State, a rivalry which would have provoked rowdy crowds even outside of the playoffs. I had managed to capture the winning goal, scored with only fourteen seconds left to play. The shot itself was impressive: the Michigan player (his name now lost to me) tottering off balance, reaching forward to make the shot before his impending crash into the boards. But it was the crowd behind the player that set the photo apart. Two guys with Michigan State jerseys were suspended forever in the middle of a long and angry, "Noooo," while the woman beside them in Michigan blue and yellow peeked through her hands, eyebrows raised and mouth open. Fans sitting right where the player was about to hit the boards pulled back, protecting themselves from the imagined impact they couldn't help but shrink from, despite the protective Plexiglas. Every single spectator, with their emotions ranging from horror to celebration, came together in one resounding image: at that moment, the game was everything.

I gazed at the photo. Sure, I could do that again...probably. True, my best lenses these days were suited more for portraits than for action shots, but I should still be able to capture some of what I had seen in that game. Portraits, hockey—at least they both involved people. In all honesty, the photo was a fluke, but I didn't have to tell anyone else that. I had been green enough to call it a fluke to my own editor at the time.

"You've got a lot to learn, girl," Connor had replied, his lips curving into a smile. "And it ain't about photography. You can't tell your editor that your best shot was a mistake."

Where was Connor these days? If anyone I knew had access to the world of sports photography, it was him. He followed the action of the games like a predator, seeking out the moments of conflict, triumph and despair on instinct. And if anyone would know how to finagle a press pass to the hockey world championships, it was Connor.

I found him in my search immediately, and as I clicked on a link to his site, I wondered why I hadn't thought to look for him before. But instead of spending my last year at the University of Michigan pursuing photojournalism, I had settled for baby portraits and Brad.

I frowned and looked up, reminding my stubborn self that I was far from Detroit. Outside the window of the café, this new city was mine for the month. But as I gazed along the sidewalk, a man caught my eye. Tall, with hulking broad shoulders, wearing sunglasses and a baseball cap pulled low over his face, mostly hiding the cut over his eye. *Niklas*. It was him. I was sure of it, but something in the way he held himself, stiff and alert, made it clear that he didn't want to be seen. He walked slowly towards the bakery, scanning the outdoor tables. No one else seemed to notice him. Then he raised his head and saw me. At least I thought he did because he stopped for a minute, his face pointed directly at me, but the sunglasses hid his eyes. I smiled a little, and I thought I saw the corners of his mouth turn up. He paused and then took a few steps in my direction. My heart skittered as I sized up the sculpted muscles of his arms. God, what was wrong with me? Yeah, he was hot, but did I need to stare each time I saw him?

But as he passed a table not far from mine, a woman grabbed his arm and said something in Swedish. Niklas muttered something back, then turned and walked away.

My ridiculous grin fell from my face. What had just happened? Had he been looking at this other woman, not me? I could feel the flush of humiliation rising. Or had he headed over to talk but changed his mind? Either way, it felt like the social equivalent of slamming the door in my face, which would make this the second time in one day. Of course no one in the building had spoken to him, as Veronica had reported. Everyone else had enough sense to stay away from this rude brute of a man. And what made my frustration flare even higher was the nagging sting of rejection—some part of me actually cared.

Deep breaths. What had I been doing before he intruded on my thoughts? It was hard to remember. I glanced down at my computer screen. Conner. Hockey. I forced my mind back to the words in front of me. I wrote a quick message, crossed my fingers and pressed send.

4
Another nice guy

I knocked on the door and fluffed up the flower bouquet I was holding. Dinner with Veronica and Filip had sounded like the makings of a good evening until Veronica mentioned that Filip had invited a friend over as well. A single, male friend. Now, as I stood outside Veronica's door, the idea of being set up with one of Filip's friends seemed even worse than it had earlier that day on the phone.

But I owed my cost-free housing in Stockholm to Veronica and Filip, and if I were totally honest with myself, without it, I would probably still be following endless internet image searches of everywhere from Mumbai to the Australian Outback, only to quickly hide them when I heard Brad's key in the door. So though I wanted nothing more than to escape back up to my apartment and close the door for the night, I willed myself to stay in place.

I knocked again. Footsteps echoed, but they weren't coming from Veronica's apartment. I glanced over my shoulder and caught a glimpse of Niklas walking up the stairs. A sudden burst of hope ran through me. Was Niklas the friend Filip had matched me with? Logically, this didn't make sense. I knew Filip and Veronica hadn't even spoken to Niklas. Still, I was hoping that, somehow, it would be him anyway.

I closed my eyes, irritated with the sudden leaps my mind was taking.

But the footsteps stopped. I opened my eyes again. Niklas took a couple steps across the landing. My heart skittered faster, and before I had the sense to stop myself, my gaze fell to his t-shirt, stretched across his broad chest and around his muscular arms, the same ones I was still sure my mind had exaggerated. But, again, this wasn't the case.

Niklas was a few feet away, watching me. He was close, distractingly close, the kind of close that made me momentarily forget why I was standing in the hallway in the first place. Close enough for me to smell his aftershave and…him.

Oh, my. His scent triggered a rush of awareness through me. Much better than beer and cigarettes. His blond hair hung over his forehead, sexy and tousled. He looked even better than he had the day before outside my apartment, if that was possible.

"Wrong floor," he said, looking amused.

I wrinkled my brow, then laughed. Niklas had assumed that I had stopped a floor too early on my way back home. "This is my friend's place."

"The other American?" he said, raising his eyebrows.

"North American," I corrected him with a smile. "She's Mexican."

"If she's the reason you're here, I guess I'll have to meet her," he murmured.

Whoa. He said this almost to himself, but his eyes were still firmly fixed on me. I had no idea how to begin to interpret his comment, especially after his attempts to avoid me only days ago. He opened his mouth to continue, but at that moment, Veronica opened the door. Quickly, he turned back to the spiral staircase and disappeared. But Veronica had seen him, too, and for once, she was silent, taking in the situation.

"Nice," she whispered as he disappeared around the corner. "It's a good thing Ludvig isn't here yet. You've definitely gotten that guy's attention, and he looks like he'd eat Ludvig for breakfast."

She pulled me inside with a soft chuckle, and we walked down the hall together.

"Filip just ran out for a couple things," she said, heading for the living room. "He should be back right about now."

The inside of their apartment was sparsely decorated, much like the one where I was staying, but Veronica's felt warmer, more like a home. Though the furniture was much the same, light gray, boxy and low to the ground, Veronica had hung a long, vivid painting of the Mexican countryside that made the room come alive. And it put me a little more at ease, despite my hesitations about the evening.

"Is that your work?" I asked.

Veronica nodded. "I painted it the last time I visited. It makes me feel like I'm closer to home."

"It's beautiful," I said, studying the long brushstrokes that drew my eye up to the volcano I recognized immediately: the Popocatépetl, looming ominously in the background.

"Sorry about tonight," said Veronica, as if she had read my thoughts through the front door. "Filip feels like we owe you for introducing us all those years ago. He wants to return the favor."

Filip and I had met in a photography class my junior year in college, but I didn't think to introduce him to Veronica until a few months before we all graduated. And when I backed out of the trip to Europe Veronica and I had fantasized about for our whole senior year, Filip had casually offered to join her instead. Though Veronica had kept the full story of what had happened on that trip vague, as far as I knew, Veronica had never looked back.

"But you already did return the favor. The apartment, I mean," I said. "That's a lot more helpful than meeting Ludvig."

Veronica smiled. "I already tried to tell that to Filip. But he was really sad to hear that you and Brad broke up. And you know how he is when he gets his mind set on something. Besides, this is the sports photography connection I was telling you about. And Ludvig is a nice guy."

I laughed. "That's just what I need. Another nice guy. Weren't you saying something about nice dentists the other day?"

Yes, Brad was nice. The kind of controlled niceness that sucked the excitement out of anything we did. Though I wasn't much for hockey, I once bought us tickets to a Detroit Red Wings game for his birthday in hopes of catching a glint of thrill behind Brad's even-tempered eyes. Maybe, I had thought, just maybe it would spark him to life.

But I had left the arena disappointed. Even I had found myself jumping out of my seat as the Red Wings forward made a last-minute breakaway goal to win the game, but Brad, a self-professed Red Wings fan, had stayed seated, smiling at the excitement around him.

"That was fun. Thanks," said Brad in a voice that held nothing more than mild amusement as we filed out of the arena, celebrations still erupting all around us.

Another nice guy? No, thanks.

"It's just dinner," said Veronica, putting her arm around me and giving me a squeeze. "Then Filip has done his duty and you both can move on."

The rattle of a key in the front door echoed through the apartment. Veronica disappeared down the hall and reappeared, accompanied by both Filip and another man.

"Caroline, this is Ludvig," she said, and Ludvig

held out his hand for a soft shake.

I had to admit that Ludvig was good-looking, though in a studied way. His hair was carefully sculpted into a messy spike in the front and neatly combed in the back. As I shook his hand, I realized I could already confirm that Veronica was right: Ludvig was nice, though maybe not in the way that Brad was. He was certainly better dressed than Brad had ever been, and there was an edge to Ludvig I couldn't read.

Filip set down the bottle of wine in his hand and whispered something in Veronica's ear. Then they both disappeared into the kitchen, leaving Ludvig and me to figure out an appropriate distance from each other on the couch. I chose the middle-left, not too intimate, but not scared of him, either. After a few shifts, Ludvig settled into the middle. Filip and Veronica emerged from the kitchen momentarily to carry in small plates and napkins and then disappeared again. The room was silent. I searched for something to say, but then Ludvig spoke first.

"Filip tells me you and he studied photography together at the University of Michigan." He spoke in measured British English. "He also said that you gave up your life back there and bought an around-the-world ticket. And you're working on a career change?"

My face heated up. Stated this plainly, my trip sounded more flaky than exciting. It felt a bit like I was sitting for an interview, and it wasn't going well.

"I'm, um, still working on the details," I said,

searching for a better spin. "I'm part of a summer article series for a magazine. We're doing interviews and photos of ex-pats around the world. I'm starting with Veronica. I have a friend in Italy and another friend in Croatia, and I'll be looking for others to interview along the way."

"Sounds adventurous," he said in a clipped tone. I didn't know how to read his expression.

"Thanks, I think," I said, smiling. "The jury is still out as to whether 'adventurous' will cross the line into 'crazy' or 'hare-brained.'"

I was trying to lighten the mood, but the effort fell flat. He was studying me intensely, taking in my whole being as I talked, as if I were putting on a performance that he was now assessing, and he didn't know how to react to it. Though his English was quite good, I found myself wondering if he hadn't followed my last sentence. But then he broke out into a smile.

"It could be a good career move if you plan to stay in some popular travel destinations. I'm sure you'll think of something," he said.

I almost laughed. He apparently thought I needed some comforting.

There were murmurs and the low rumble of laughter from down the hall. Then Veronica and Filip reappeared carrying wine glasses and another platter, this one full of olives, grapes and cheeses. Filip arranged two armchairs next to the low table and offered one to Veronica before he sat down.

"Has Ludvig told you yet that he's one of the most sought-after sports photographers in Sweden?" said Filip with a mischievous smile.

I shook my head. I turned to Ludvig, and his expression was almost smug.

"I've had a lot of success over the years." He smiled at me and then seemed to realize that the situation called for a little more humility. "I didn't make it into the top hockey league here in Sweden, so photographing it seemed like the next best thing," he added with a wry smile. His words were flippant, but behind them, I thought I detected a hint of bitterness. "You'd think with the last name Sundin, I'd get a little more ice time."

I stared at him blankly, and Filip laughed.

"Mats Sundin, Caroline," he said gently. "A famous Swedish hockey player, though apparently not so famous over in the U.S."

I blushed. If this guy could get me passes to the hockey tournament, I certainly needed to make a better impression.

"Sorry," I said. "I guess you're talking to the wrong person. My experience is with college hockey." *And even then it wasn't voluntarily.* I decided to keep that last part to myself. Instead, I sat back and listened as the conversation switched over to stories from our pasts. Veronica was the center of attention, as always.

I sat back and admired my friend as she spoke. Sweden was far from Mexico in every way possible, and yet Veronica seemed to be very happy here. She had left behind a gaggle of sisters and cousins as well as the warm weather and sun. The only parts of Mexico left in her daily life were her paintings, hanging on the walls of her decidedly un-Mexican apartment.

For most of our years at the University of Michigan, I had assumed that Veronica would head back to Mexico after we graduated, trading the icy winters for the ease of the upper-class future her parents had planned for her. But as we went into our senior year, something shifted. While I quietly scaled back my own plans, telling myself that I'd travel with Brad when he was ready, Veronica's world seemed to open up. She didn't want to go back to Mexico, not yet at least.

After reluctantly giving up on me as a travel partner, Veronica set off with jobless and decidedly un-Catholic Filip, scandalizing her family and effectively cutting off any hope of a good marriage back in Puebla. As far as I knew, Veronica didn't regret that decision at all. Back in Michigan, I had often tried to imagine what my life would have been like if I had set off with Veronica. It certainly would have changed both our lives, though looking at my friend's life with Filip now, it was hard to imagine that Veronica would have been better for it. But what had once felt like adventure had increasingly seemed more like an abyss of uncertainty for me. And, after all, Brad was unfailingly nice. And Catholic, or nominally so. At least my parents were glad for that.

Filip had said something to me, bringing me out of my thoughts.

"Sorry—what was that?"

Filip laughed. "I asked if you've ever been to Spain."

I shook my head. "This is my first time outside of North America."

"I'm working at the European soccer championships," said Ludvig in the same, understated tone. "They're in Spain later this month. It's going to be big."

"As a photographer?"

Ludvig nodded.

I wondered how he had found his way into a photography career with that kind of assignment, the kind that made real money. I searched his face for hints of his age. He certainly looked a bit older than I was but not enough to solely explain his position. It had to be ambition, I guessed, if first impressions meant anything.

"But we don't have anyone on our team that speaks Spanish," he continued.

Both Veronica and Filip were looking at me.

"Me?" I looked from one to the other. "No, my Spanish is terrible. You know that." I rolled my eyes at Veronica.

And this wasn't modesty speaking. Despite all my years of Spanish classes, the only time I had actually been forced to use my Spanish was on my family's one and only trip to Mexico. I always spoke English to my father, even when he spoke Spanish back to me. Now, I regretted not trying a little harder when I was younger, but it was too late. As Veronica had pointed out more than once, I sounded like a *gringa* stuck in elementary school.

"Your Spanish is just terrible for someone whose father is Mexican," laughed Veronica. "You could definitely get by in Spain."

"You sure know how to flatter a girl," I said, giving her a wry smile. "But I'm still working on hockey passes."

"For the world championships this week?" asked Ludvig.

"Yes. But I have some leads," I quickly added. The last thing I wanted was to sound desperate for a job. And my statement was kind-of true. I had an idea for a lead, though Connor hadn't responded to my email yet.

"I'm going to a couple of the games. I know some people who work in media at The Globe. I can check into getting you a pass if you'd like," he said, and for the first time that night, he sounded earnest. "If you give me your number, I'll get back to you tomorrow."

I knew I should accept his offer, though the idea left me vaguely uneasy. Still, I put on a good smile and thanked him. Then I watched as Filip gave Veronica a look that seemed to say, *I told you so*.

5
"Afraid I'll grab you again?"

There was something about the feel of the early morning hours that kept me waking up every day for solitary walks, with only my camera and my pepper spray in hand, despite what had happened the other day. Logically, I knew that I'd never adjust to the time change if I kept getting up at 3:30 am for a walk, only to crash back into bed after a couple of hours, just as the city began to wake up. But I couldn't help it. I had found a way to have Stockholm all to myself. In this magical world of mine, I was finally able to live inside the stillness of one of my photographs, able to move through its world as slowly as I wanted, without disruption.

I tried to let the memory of the other night, Baseball Cap and the pepper spray clutched tightly in my hand, fade. The occasional wanderers passed by. Sometimes an amorous couple, but mostly groups of drunk teenagers or men far beyond the teen years but still drunk. They didn't come near. Instead, they continued in loud, testosterone-fueled voices until they disappeared around the corner, oblivious to the hazy glow of the morning light on the leaves of the park trees.

I only had a few more minutes before the sun emerged, changing everything. I removed the lens cap and pointed the camera up through the magnolia tree branches in front of me, the pink and white blossoms soft against the clear morning sky.

Suddenly, my arms prickled with goose bumps. Someone was there. I hadn't heard anyone approach, yet I could feel the presence of another person. Close. Too close. My heart pounded in my ears as I lowered my camera and turned around.

Niklas. He was standing only a few feet away, near enough to make my heart jump, though I now wasn't sure if this was the surprise of his sudden presence or the way I had sized him up before I was even aware of what I was doing. He was dressed in a t-shirt and shorts that barely contained his sizable body, and a considerable portion of this body was muscle. The cut over his eye had healed a little. Though his gaze was as impassive as ever, his cheeks were flushed, and his mouth was parted in what looked like surprise.

"What are *you* doing out here?" he asked softly.

"Exactly what it looks like," I said. I sounded a little more curt than I had intended, so I softened my voice. "I'm photographing the trees in the park. I just didn't realize you were so...so near."

My face heated up. His eyes bore into me as I said

these last two words, and for a moment, his guarded look faltered.

"I meant what are you doing out here, alone again at four in the morning?"

"It's when the light is best," I said with a twinge of irritation. Why was I explaining myself to this man? I put a hand on my hip and, with a hint of sass, added, "What are you doing out here?"

He ignored my question. "It's not safe to be out here by yourself."

I raised my eyebrows, bristling at his stark tone and the implication that he, practically a stranger, was the authority on what was best for me. And he was implying that I wasn't safe out here when he himself was, in fact, out here alone as well. After all the talk about pro-gender-equity men in Sweden, how had I managed to find a neighbor who hadn't gotten the message? I sighed.

"I have pepper spray," I said, digging in my pocket until I pulled it out.

"Not sure that stuff is legal here in Sweden," he said, raising an eyebrow. "Besides, you weren't ready to use it."

"I would have been if there was real danger."

I knew my answer sounded childish before the words even left my mouth, but I said it anyway. Much to my increasing irritation, he gave a dry laugh.

"Fine," he said. "Then spray me. Right now."

I frowned. "You don't want me to do that. It'll burn

your eyes. Badly."

"That reasoning is why the pepper spray won't help you," he said, the amusement still on his face. "You have to be willing to use it."

He was goading me, I could feel it, but it was working. My hand twitched around the canister.

"Fine," I said and reached to pull the cap off the spray.

But before I even touched it, he grabbed both of my hands together with one of his. He used the other to turn me around and hold me against his solid chest. My pepper spray dropped to the ground. I gasped, my mind trying to process the sensation of my back against the warmth of his hard muscles. I stopped breathing. His large arm held me firmly against him, and my heart frantically pounded inside my chest. I looked down at the scarred knuckles of the hand that was easily holding both of mine.

Before my mind had fully registered all these details, his grip softened. Gently, he turned me back around by my waist so I was facing him, but he didn't release me right away. I wasn't sure where to look. At the broad, solid chest only inches away? At the tense muscles of his arms? I drew in my first, shaky breath in too long. I tilted my head up and found his eyes fixed on mine.

"It's not safe to wander around alone at night, even if it's light out," he said softly.

Though he didn't move, I had the sudden,

inexplicable feeling that Niklas was about to kiss me. I parted my lips in anticipation. But I blinked and the feeling was gone. The warmth of his large hands disappeared. Niklas picked up my pepper spray from the ground and placed it back in my hand. His fingers lingered on mine before he pulled them away and whispered, "It's especially not safe if you're not ready to use this."

"I still think I could have been," I said, though my voice no longer held the defiance it had just minutes ago. I took a deep breath, trying to rein in my thoughts, which had quickly galloped out of control. My heart rate was still nowhere near normal yet, and the fact that his body was only inches from mine wasn't helping.

Niklas looked at me carefully. Then he gave a laugh and shook his head. "Can I walk you home?"

"I'm not ready to go yet," I grumbled. "I still have a few more minutes before the sun comes up."

"I'm not in a hurry," he said, sitting down on a large stone, not waiting for my reply.

I turned back to the magnolia tree, trying hard to put Niklas out of my mind. My hands were still shaking, and the heat of his body lingered, tingling down my back. But what unsettled me most was my own response to him. I should have been scared by the sudden nearness of his body just a few minutes before, but I wasn't. Quite the opposite, in fact.

Who was this man? I felt a strong pull between us, though more than once he had suddenly turned rude and ignored me. Now he was going out of his way to make sure I was safe. Again. Whoever he was, he was certainly in great shape. I glanced over at him again, my gaze sliding over the long, thick muscles of his thighs. What did he want from me? Niklas sat silently on the rock, his back towards me, but I could feel him there, even when I turned away.

Sighing, I replaced my lens cap. "I'm ready."

"You don't have to rush," he said, sounding surprised.

"No," I said. "I can't concentrate."

"Afraid I'll grab you again?" he said with mock-seriousness.

I laughed. It was difficult to stay annoyed at him, and the charming lilt of Swedish in his words wasn't helping.

"Come on," I said, rolling my eyes, and we started back towards the apartment building. I could feel him next to me, close, before he spoke.

"So you must come from one of those small towns where no one locks their doors?"

I chuckled. "Actually, I'm from Detroit."

Niklas gave me a funny look I couldn't read.

I added, "You know, Detroit, Michigan? Middle of the U.S., the state with all the lakes around it? Up by Canada."

He furrowed his eyebrows and nodded. "Yeah, I know where Detroit is."

There was a moment of quiet while I tried,

unsuccessfully, to interpret his tone. Then I gave up.

"I'm not helpless, you know," I said suddenly. "I took a self-defense class back in college, and we practiced on each other a lot. But not with anyone as quick or...as big as you." The flush was creeping into my face again.

Niklas stopped and turned me by my shoulders so I was facing him. His intense eyes were fixed on me, sending a fresh wave of awareness through me. "I wasn't trying to say that you're helpless. I'm saying you weren't ready to protect yourself. And you know that there are real threats out here."

He didn't have to say more; the implication was clear. Whoever he was with the other morning in the park might not have left me alone. This time I didn't answer. He was right; I wasn't ready. When I looked through the view finder of my camera, everything else fell away. But what was I supposed to do with that information? Stay inside when this beautiful, quiet park waited right outside my window?

He let his hands brush down my arms as they returned to his sides. Everything about our interactions felt so intimate, despite the fact that we barely knew each other. Niklas turned back along the park path. We walked in silence as the first rays of morning light shone through the trees. The rustle of the wind, birds, our shoes tapping a quiet rhythm on the path; these were the only sounds. The rest of the city slept as Niklas and I walked over the hill, back to where our building was visible. My *magical world*, I had called this spot. It felt different with Niklas there, but it was no less magical, I had to admit.

"I'm sorry," Niklas said suddenly. "I imagine you wanted to be alone back there. But it's not just what happened the other morning. There was an attack in the park not so long ago. A group of guys out at night, looking for fights. And worse."

"Is that what happened to you?" I asked.

Niklas touched the cut above his eyebrow. It had faded beneath the strips but was still pink.

"This?" He chuckled. "No, this fight wasn't in the park."

I didn't know what to think of his answer. He hadn't refuted my reference to a fight, only the location. What kind of grown man gets into a fight? The not-a-good-idea kind of man. I stole another glance at Niklas. He had a scar up his knee as well. Another fight? He was clearly built for it, and his ability to disarm me so quickly suggested...well, what did it suggest? All I could think about was the way the hard muscles of his chest and arms had felt pressed against me.

My face reddened as I realized that Niklas was watching my eyes move along his body. Again. And he was smiling. Determined not to let myself get flustered, I tried the question I had asked earlier.

"What are you doing out here at four in the morning?"

"Jogging. It helps when I can't sleep. And it's nice

to have the city to myself sometimes."

I nodded. I knew exactly what he meant, though walking with him hadn't turned out so badly, either.

We crossed the empty street and stopped in front of our tall, stone building. I licked my lips, trying to anticipate the next turn that this meeting would take. I had to give him credit; Niklas was anything but boring so far.

"Thanks for walking me home. Really," I said with a little smile, and he nodded. "Are you coming in?"

Niklas shook his head. "I'm going out for a run."

"Alone?" I said in mock-horror.

"Unless you're coming."

There was something in his voice, a mix of humor and intimacy, almost as if the invitation were a dare, though I wasn't exactly sure what the dare was.

I shook my head, though at the moment the idea of spending a little more time with him had its appeal.

"If you want to go out tomorrow morning again, knock on my door. I'll be up." Then his mouth quirked up into a hint of a smile. "And I promise not to make any sudden grabs at you next time."

I met his eyes and felt my heart take off again, the memory of his body against mine rushing through me. His eyes truly were the color of the sky that morning, light and clear against his broad cheekbones but with an intensity that made everything else around us fade into the background. He had shaved this time, which made him look different, less Viking brute, more...well, if I were totally honest with myself, more very sexy guy. A rude, sexy guy who comes home smelling like beer and stale cigarettes with bad taste in friends and a habit of getting into fights.

Niklas was studying me, his smile fading as if he could tell what I was thinking. I swallowed. He opened his mouth as if he were on the verge of saying something, but then he seemed to think better of it.

"See you," he said abruptly and jogged back across the street, picking up his pace as he entered the park.

I watched him disappear into the trees and then looked up at the building. A new wave of irritation washed over me as I realized that Niklas had successfully maneuvered me back to the apartment building, cutting my morning session short. And I wasn't going back. It was the kind of subtle control that Brad had tried to exert over me all those years, though I had to admit that Niklas had done it a lot more skillfully. And enticingly. But I also couldn't deny my irritation at the fact that I had so easily let myself get sidetracked by this man. Even if he was probably right: I shouldn't be out alone at night.

6
Can you know a person through a photograph?

"If you're staying in Sweden for a month, you should at least try Swedish foods," said Veronica, holding up a jar of something floating in a mysterious yellow sauce.

"In principle, I agree with you, but I think I have to draw the line here," I said, eyeing the jar with skepticism. "What is that?"

"Herring pickled in mustard sauce," said Veronica with a smile.

"Really?" I took the jar to examine it for myself. "Pickled fish with mustard? That sounds both exotic and repelling. Maybe that's reason enough to try it."

"Or how about this one?" said Veronica, grabbing another jar off the store shelf—an entire shelf lined with identical little fish jars in various sauces. The one she now held was white and creamy. "Garlic," Veronica translated off the label.

"Which disguises the herring flavor the most?" I asked. Seeing the look of exasperation on my friend's face, I put the mustard jar into my basket.

The grocery store was surprisingly well-stocked,

especially considering its unassuming entranceway on the edge of the enormous St. Eriksplan traffic circle. Everything inside was smaller than I was used to, from the little rectangular packages of milk to the mini bottles of soda, stacked high in crates. The exception was the cheese: enormous wedges and rounds took up a good portion of the refrigerator section, all white and with holes. Could there possibly be this many versions of Swiss cheese?

"Am I done yet? I think I have as much as I can carry," I said as I grabbed two bags of pasta off the shelf, thankful that at least these were recognizable.

"So he snuck up on you while you were taking photos?" asked Veronica as we got in line for the cashier.

"Not exactly snuck up. He was trying to see if I was ready to fight off an attack. And, of course, I wasn't."

"He sounds a little creepy. And then there's the way he grunts at everyone in the building. He's home at all sorts of odd hours. Doesn't he have a job?"

I laughed. "You've certainly been watching him carefully."

"Well, he *is* really hot, too," said Veronica, chuckling.

"Are married women supposed to say things like that?"

"If they haven't gone blind. Don't get me wrong. Filip is more than enough for me. But that doesn't change the fact that this guy Niklas is hot enough to model underwear. And he was staring at you in the hallway with more than just the weather on his mind the other day."

The woman in front of us glared over her shoulder and then turned back around, making me laugh even harder.

Veronica shook her head and whispered, "I told you I'm the loudest woman in this country."

I had to smile. Veronica didn't seem to care, but she continued at a more muted volume. "Just because he's hot doesn't make it a good idea to start something with him."

"I'm not here to start something with him, or with anyone, for that matter," I said, letting out a sigh as I loaded my groceries onto the register counter. "The only thing I'm after right now is a new direction in my career, one that's finally within reach. I just need to figure out the finances part. I don't want to think about Brad, cutesy babies, contrived wedding poses, or a new guy who distracts me from what I want to do."

The look on Veronica's face told me that my words had come out a little sharper than I meant them to.

"Sorry," I added, squeezing Veronica's arm. "As you can tell, I'm still a little sensitive. Want to know the last thing my father said to me before I left? 'You'll never find yourself a husband if you run off like this.' Like of all the reasons I should or shouldn't take an around-the-world trip, finding a husband should be at the top of the list."

"*Dios mio*, Caroline," said Veronica with half a smile. "You were leaving steady Brad, with his lawyer salary and his BMW. Your father is Mexican, and you're his only daughter."

"What about your Mexican father? What did he say when you left?"

Veronica rolled her eyes. "My Mexican father has four other daughters who are much more compliant than I am."

Both Veronica and I burst out laughing as we walked out of the grocery store and onto St. Eriksplan.

"I miss laughing like this," said Veronica. "Even when I try to hold myself back here in Sweden, I still get stares. For a country so concerned with gender equity, Swedish women certainly keep their behavior under control."

"And I don't?"

Veronica shook her head. "At least not when we were in college."

But the person I had been back then felt far, far away. I frowned. "I'm not sure if that's a compliment or not."

"Definitely a compliment."

As the door swung open into my temporary home, my phone gave a quiet ding. I searched my purse and finally pulled it out. I read the message twice.

"What should I do about this?" I asked, showing Veronica the cell phone she had lent me during my stay.

Still interested in hockey passes?
You can come with me. /Ludvig

"What do you mean?" said Veronica, raising her eyebrows. "Isn't that what you wanted?"

I wrinkled my nose. "If you mean the tickets, yes. But doesn't that sound like a date?"

"So what if it is? A date isn't a promise of anything else except your time that evening. Besides, you can at least give him a chance."

My eyes narrowed. "Did you set this up?"

Veronica looked back at me and laughed. "No, but I may have talked you up to him a little. Maybe."

I put my phone back into my bag and sighed as we carried the grocery bags into the kitchen.

"This apartment is beautiful, though I'm not sure I could ever get used to living here," I said as I unloaded the little rectangular cartons of milk into the refrigerator.

"I've found that, under the right conditions, you get used to just about anything," said Veronica with a smile. "Can I wander through? I'll never get to see my neighbors' flat otherwise."

"Of course."

I laid out the foods that had been identified as sandwich ingredients and then opened the door that led out onto a tiny balcony.

"You brought these along?" Veronica's voice

floated through the door.

I followed the voice and found my friend in my bedroom. Veronica was looking at the long table underneath the tall windows where I had laid out my most precious photographs.

"You brought them?" said Veronica with a laugh that seemed to be a mixture of incredulity and admiration. "You had only one suitcase to travel around the world, and you brought the photographs?"

"I couldn't leave them. I don't know how long I'll be gone. That's why I only have two pairs of shoes," I said. "And no jackets."

We both sat on the edge of the apartment's enormous king-sized bed and looked at the pictures. They certainly weren't the best photos I had ever taken, and many of them had faded in their frames after years of exposure, but I had held onto these photos for the stories they captured so many years ago.

"I thought you were a little nutty the first day we met," said Veronica, smiling. "You didn't unpack anything except for those photos for the first week of college."

"I wasn't planning to stay in that room. We were in North Quad. I wanted to move onto the main campus with my friends."

"But just the photos? No clothes or even a toothbrush?" Veronica's smile turned into a chuckle.

"Just to be clear, I did brush my teeth that first week," I said with a smirk. "But, yes, just the photos stayed out."

The photos were of Mexico, on the one and only trip I had taken there with my family. While my other friends from school visited exciting places like Acapulco and Cancun, my parents and I went to Puebla, nowhere near beaches. The only point of interest was an enormous volcano called the Popocatepetl that spewed threatening smoke for my entire visit.

Mexico didn't look anything like the photos of paradise I had seen. It was dusty and hot, with a kind of poverty lurking around each corner that I had never seen before. To my surprise and embarrassment, my own mother, a blond-haired Texas native, spoke better Spanish than I did. It was at this point that I realized the mistake of my stubborn refusal to speak Spanish back to my father. I wouldn't have found the language difficult and embarrassing forever, judging from my mother's skills.

But I remembered Mexico less as a visit to a foreign country and more as the location of my first real understanding of my gruff, stoic father as a person. Even now, years later, I still had a visceral reaction to the photos I had taken at the house where my father was born.

Four generations of the family lived together in two, bougainvillea-lined houses in configurations I never fully figured out. My aunts fussed over me and asked me questions, one after another, using words that my middle-school Spanish classes hadn't covered. After a while, I'd slip out to wander around the land by myself.

One day I saw my father out, alone. I ducked behind a tree and watched him wander the property, taking in what he, the family's hope, had bought for them. I followed my father to where he sat on a tree stump, elbows leaning on his knees, staring at the old, dilapidated house where he was born. I didn't take his picture that day.

But in one attempt to capture the Popocatepetl in the distance, I had taken the photograph that I had kept hidden all these years. It was tucked away, inside a frame, behind another, more standard picture of my family, posed together by the creek. I had never shown the photo to my father, but I had handled it enough so that the edges were bent. In the corner of the photo, my father's face was filled with grief and frustration, his eyes closed at the touch of my mother's hand on the back of his neck. Though I had studied the photos over the years for clues, I was never sure what lay behind my father's unexpected emotions that day.

My mother had given me all of the pieces of my father's history before, but I had never quite figured out how to fit them together into the person I knew. For the first time, my father's bursts of emotion, if still not predictable, at least seemed to have a reason behind them.

I leaned forward and squinted at the row of faded photos in front of me. Then I turned back to Veronica.

"Do you believe you can know a person through a photograph?"

"Maybe," said Veronica. "At least a part of a person. Maybe if you catch the right moment, a part they keep to themselves comes out. Is that why you've kept these photos close all these years?"

I sighed and lay back onto the bed.

"Both my parents would have been happier if I had become a doctor. They thought the photography thing would pass," I laughed. "But something about photos, about being able to hold onto a piece of time, a piece of someone... I'm not sure why that idea is so intriguing to me, but I want to follow it. Now that I'm halfway around the world with a job that doesn't even come close to paying my expenses, I'm sure everyone thinks I'm completely crazy."

"Not really. I'm more curious about why you really stayed with Brad in the first place," Veronica said gently.

I sighed. "I don't know. He was older and seemed to have everything together, and I thought that's what I needed. You remember the guys I dated before him, right? A lot rougher and certainly not together. Toby was straight-out wild. After him, I knew I needed to do something different."

"Out of the frying pan and into the fire? Or maybe the slow-cooker is more appropriate for Brad?" said Veronica with a little snort.

"That implies heat." The corners of my mouth

pulled up a little. Only Veronica could make me laugh in the middle of a conversation like this.

"So what got you to leave that suburban paradise?"

I shrugged. "Someone sent me a link to the magazine job as a joke, a 'wouldn't this be nice' kind of thing. I didn't tell Brad I applied, and I didn't even tell him at first when I got the position. This might sound terrible, but it felt good to keep something this big from him. I still hadn't really made the connection that it wasn't just the job. That I wanted to be in control of where my life was headed."

"And what did Brad say when you told him that? I'm sure that's a bit of a hard truth to hear."

I winced at the memory of his expression. Shock was what I had seen more than anything else. Not regret or sadness or longing.

"He told me that I was making a big mistake. That I didn't appreciate all the things I had. That I wouldn't make it on my own," I said. I was quiet for a moment, and then I continued. "You know, at first, I had hoped he would come travel with me. When I told him, part of me had hoped that he would welcome the chance to give up everything and follow me, change our lives together. That he would finally show a little passion. In a way, I guess I was testing him."

"And when he didn't pass the test?"

I rubbed my forehead, trying to ease the worry lines that were creasing my forehead. "To be honest, I guess I was a little relieved."

Veronica sat down on the bed and gave me a tight squeeze around my shoulders.

"I'm glad he didn't come," said Veronica. "Then you wouldn't be here right now."

Most of the time, I felt like that, too.

REBECCA HUNTER

7
My most valuable possession hit the step
with a crack

I found the early morning gray of the apartment's hallway surprisingly cheerful. It was 3:37 am, and once again, I was wide awake. What could have been explained as jet lag last week had now turned into bad sleeping habits—up late, hoping that pushing myself to the point of exhaustion would help me sleep through the night, only to awaken around 2:30 am once again, my body whispering *I'm hungry* or *It's light out. Why not get up? Stockholm won't last forever.*

Veronica had told me more than once that if I wanted to adjust to the time, I had to stop taking naps in the middle of the day and stop eating breakfast at three in the morning. And Veronica would know, too, an expert at recovering from jet lag after four years of expat life. But truthfully, I was enjoying my odd schedule. I was awake at the most peaceful time of the day.

I threw on some clothes, grabbed my keys and pepper spray from the hall table, and then stopped, staring at the little canister in my hand. Veronica had confirmed what Niklas had suggested: It was illegal to carry pepper spray in Sweden. How I had gotten it past customs without me or the police noticing the infraction was a mystery, but I wasn't interested in breaking the law in a foreign country. I had heard stories about detentions, fines and even the loss of fingers, all out of the reach of US law. Though I was fairly sure none of these news stories that had stuck in my head were about Sweden, the threat still hovered ominously. I put the pepper spray back down on the hall table and opened the door.

Niklas's door waited for me across the dark hallway. He had told me to knock. He would walk with me and...what then? The idea of having an escort to follow me while I wandered in the park sounded worse the more I thought about it, even if that escort was exceptionally hot. In fact, my budding infatuation with him was all the more reason not to knock if I wanted to concentrate on taking photos.

I sighed and closed my door a little harder than I had intended to. Then I turned around again toward his apartment. With my pepper spray, I had felt a certain comfort walking alone in these morning hours, but without it, I was even less sure that this was a good idea. And though I had sounded confident the day before, the self-defense class Veronica and I had taken in college was hazy by now at best. Niklas had made it clear that I was nowhere near prepared to defend myself. But instead of fear, I felt my pulse quicken at the thought of Niklas's demonstration.

My frustration built as I walked over to the staircase. I took a step down and stopped. I shouldn't go out alone. Common sense told me I shouldn't be wandering around the park at night.

But restlessness tugged at me, too, begging me to get out. Finally, I closed my eyes and told myself to go now, before I changed my mind again. Or before Niklas discovered me, lingering outside his door.

Of course, moments later, I could see the obvious flaws in this sequence of events. I wasn't watching where I was going. And the stair my foot was aiming for wasn't quite as wide as I remembered it. By the time I looked down, it was too late: My foot had landed on the very edge of the step, and I tripped and flailed, searching for something to hold onto. My keys flew out of my hand, hitting the glass pane in the stairwell window before clattering to the ground. As my body fell forward, I grabbed the only thing in reach, the railing of the stairs. And my camera smacked against the wall.

Then the building was silent again as I hung from the railing, stunned. I pulled myself up, searching for my keys. But when I put tentative weight on my ankle, it gave an angry throb. Better to sit for a minute. I lowered myself onto the step, rubbing my arm. Aside from my ankle and a tugging strain at my wrist, I seemed to have survived the stumble relatively uninjured. But the smack of my camera still rang in my ears, and I took it off my neck to inspect it.

Footsteps. Just as I was about to push the power button of my camera, from behind me, a door opened. Even before I turned around, I knew it was Niklas. I smoothed the jumble of curls, sticking out everywhere, trying to look less like someone who had just tripped down the stairs.

"Was that your idea of knocking?" asked Niklas with a smirk, sitting down next to me. He was dressed in a t-shirt, shorts and running shoes again, and the long, bare muscles of his arms and legs were only inches from me now. "Are you okay?"

The staircase was narrow, and as he turned to look at me, his hand brushed up against my leg, awakening my body in the stillness between us. I wasn't even looking at him now, but the feeling was there again, the pull between us. My pulse was racing, and I took a soft, slow breath to calm it.

"I might have broken my camera," I said, pressing the power button. Nothing happened. I could feel his eyes on me as I opened a compartment at the bottom of the camera. I dumped out the batteries and then reinserted them, trying to stop my hands from shaking. Then I pressed the power button again. This time the screen lit up.

"Nice," he said. The warmth of his breath caressed my neck as he looked over my shoulder. He was so close, and I wondered if he could see how nervous he was making me. The thump of my heart had to be loud enough for him to hear, and I had to consciously steady my breath again. Niklas hovered over me, only inches away.

"That's just the first step," I said. My voice sounded surprisingly natural, considering the thoughts going through my head. "Now I need to see if I broke my lens."

What happened next I would replay in my mind many times over the next weeks. And each time, I wondered if this single event changed my life's course. What would have happened if Niklas hadn't broken my camera? Would things have turned out differently between us? But in the end, he broke it.

I took the lens cap off and jokingly pointed the camera in his direction. But instead of smiling, his face turned stony. He put up his hand to block the lens, knocking the camera out of my hand. I watched as my most valuable possession hit the step below with a crack.

We both froze.

"Shit," Niklas muttered.

Slowly, I reached down to pick up the camera. My hands shook as I pushed the power button. Nothing happened. His breath was rough in my ear as I turned the camera over, reinserted the batteries, and tried the power button again. Still nothing. Niklas was looming next to me, and the tension between us had turned into something more complicated.

"Shit," I said with a shaky laugh, trying to hold back my tears. I cradled the broken camera in my hands, not wanting to look over at Niklas again, whose gaze seemed to still be fixed on my camera—and me.

"I'm so sorry, Caroline," he said softly. The tenderness in his voice when he said my name released something inside, and the first tear rolled down my cheek. Quickly, I wiped it away.

"I wasn't thinking. I…" He seemed to be struggling with his words. "I don't like having my picture taken, and I just reacted."

"That's okay," I said automatically, still looking down. But it really didn't feel okay at all.

Niklas shook his head. "No, it's not. I'll get it fixed for you."

He lifted the camera out of my hands to inspect it. Then he gave it back to me and paused, holding his large, scarred hands around mine. For that moment, with his fingers on my skin, I did feel a little better. Then he pulled away.

"Wait here," he said. He stood up and headed back into his apartment.

It was only after Niklas disappeared through his door that I let my eyes overflow. My camera was the center of my life, the reason I was here. Without a way to take photos, the career door the magazine series opened for me would slam shut. They wouldn't give me a second chance if I backed out now. Without a camera, I was a broke traveler, a little too far past college to be without a plan. Adventure, career, happiness—the camera was at the center of all of this. And I couldn't afford another one, certainly not another like the one I was cradling in my hand.

Niklas's footsteps echoed through his apartment and out into the hallway. I wiped the tears that had fallen down my cheeks, not ready to expose just how much this hurt.

Niklas sat down next to me again, even closer than before. His leg leaned lightly against mine, and he put a warm hand on my back. His body was so near to mine, and his breaths were quiet, uneven. In his other hand, he held a small black bag, which he set in my lap. A camera bag. Another tear fell, and Niklas reached over to wipe it away. My breath was shaky.

"I know it's not the same thing as having your own, but please take mine for now, while I get yours fixed."

I shook my head. "It's all right. I can take mine into a shop. You can keep yours."

What I didn't say was that I wasn't going to let my camera out of my sight, especially not with the man who just knocked it onto the stone steps. Besides, cameras weren't interchangeable. Mine wasn't anything like the one someone with a passing interest in photography would buy. Just the lens itself was worth two months of my salary back in Michigan.

Niklas shook his head, and I could feel his hand tense on my back.

"Look," he said, putting his other hand on my arm,

"I don't know much about cameras, but the guy I bought it from told me this was a good one. I bought a few lenses, too, when I thought I'd try some photography a year or so ago, but now I'm not sure what any of them do."

The heat of both his hands rushed through me, muddling my thoughts and melting some of my frustration. I closed my eyes, unleashing a flood of images that had nothing to do with cameras. Images of him pulling me against him the way he had in the park, but with an entirely different purpose this time. I pushed them away. I opened my eyes again and looked down at his camera bag, trying to gather my thoughts.

I unzipped it and took a deep breath. Then I pulled his camera out with a small gasp. This wasn't an amateur camera; in fact, it was nicer than my own. I had read extensively about this particular model, but I could never justify the price tag. Not for baby photos in the mall studio, at least.

"I—I can't take this," I finally said. "I don't have the money to replace it if it breaks." This was an understatement. If mine cost two months of my Michigan salary, this one cost six, neither of which I had right now.

Niklas ran his hand through his hair. His eyes were on me again as I gently turned his camera over in my hands. Each of his breaths met the bare skin of my neck. He drew in a deeper breath as if to speak, then reconsidered.

Finally, he said, "It's a year old, and I've only used it once. Right now it's worth nothing to me because I can't work it. Try it out and then show me how to use it. You'll be doing me a favor."

Whether or not he really considered this a favor was a bit suspect, but I couldn't ignore the fact that this was a chance to try out my dream camera, the one that had never been within reach in Michigan. And it also meant I was no longer out of a career.

I set his camera carefully back into the bag and zipped it closed. "So tell me again what you're doing with a camera like this."

"Trying to find myself a productive hobby?" he attempted a half smile. His voice was soft and tender, and he was watching me closely.

Though I still had an uneasy feeling about what kind of problems I could be creating by agreeing to this exchange, I couldn't deny I wanted to take it. And then there was another, uncomfortable pulse of excitement at the idea that this would be a connection between us. As bad of an idea as this was, I wanted a reason to see him again.

"Okay," I said before I could change my mind again. I turned over my own camera to pop out the memory card and then handed it over to him. "I'll try it out. Thank you."

We both moved to stand, and I realized too late that the staircase was too narrow for us both to do this at the same time. And now more than just his hand was touching me. He was facing me, and his leg pressed against mine. His eyes were just as intense as they had been early the other morning, and they seemed to be asking me something.

Whatever it was, the answer was yes.

His hand rested softly against the curve of my hips. I turned my body toward him, and he came even closer. His breaths were harsh and uneven as he stood over me. I didn't lift my own hand to smooth his hair the way I wanted to. I still wasn't sure what was happening between us.

"I'm really sorry about your camera," he said. His eyes stayed on mine, and he reached up with his other hand to brush my hair over my shoulder.

"I came out here to…" He broke off and shook his head instead. "I'm just sorry."

He stroked further down my back, and my heart pounded wildly. Were we about to kiss? It was a strange question, but, somehow, I could feel that he wanted to. I wanted it, too.

"It's okay," I said, and this time I really meant it.

I lowered my gaze to his t-shirt, stretched over his broad shoulders and across the muscles of his chest. He smelled of contrasts, the clean scent of soap mingled with something much more basic. I wanted to touch him. Slowly, I brought my hand up and let it rest against his side. His muscles twitched, and a small groan escaped from his mouth. My hand trembled as I felt hard muscles and heat through his t-shirt. I looked back up into his eyes. What I found there was the same want and hunger I felt simmering inside myself.

He leaned down and let his lips brush against my mouth once, twice, before he parted his lips and gently took mine.

The kiss was soft and warm, a question, *please?*

Yes, I told him with my lips, and he urged my mouth wider. *Yes*, I told him again, and his tongue stroked mine. Then I was reaching for him, the muscles of his back, his sides, with his camera bag hanging precariously from my elbow.

His hand wove into my hair, pulling me deeper into the kiss. His other hand moved down to cup my rear, pulling my body against his. The camera bag dropped. It didn't matter. There was no mistaking his arousal, and my own body responded unequivocally, without waiting for my brain, moving, pressing harder against him. Everything was urgent, and I had to touch him. I wanted more. Each part of my body awakened as he touched me, each muscle tightening.

Then, as suddenly as it began, he broke away, leaving us both gasping.

"*Gud*, I shouldn't have done that," he muttered.

I just stared at him, too stunned to say anything.

"Sorry," he added, though I wasn't sure what this sorry was for. If it was for the kiss, there was certainly no need for an apology.

Now Niklas wasn't looking at me at all. Instead, he picked up my camera and disappeared down the spiral staircase, taking two steps at a time.

I leaned back against the stone wall, my breaths coming fast, trying to process the events that had all taken place these last minutes in this hallway. The heat of his hands lingered on my skin, and I could still feel his fingers flexing on my rear as he pulled me closer, wanting more. But as my mind began to catch up with my body, the exquisite tenderness of his first kiss, a tenderness that had quickly lit into something much more, mixed the sinking feeling that kissing Niklas— and everything else I had wanted in the moment— wasn't a good idea at all.

He was my neighbor, making this entanglement much too close to home, especially if things turned sour. And that seemed likely, considering how quickly he took off. Again. Despite the care I had seen from him so far, I knew he had another side. I had heard him that night when I arrived, late, probably assuming no one else was awake. Or not caring. At least I had thought it was him, yelling what could only be curses in Swedish that pulsed through the apartment walls between us.

I knew better than to get involved with someone like that. I knew that those emotions could twist into something darker. From time to time, my father's gruff and quiet demeanor spilled over into something less controlled. And I had watched my mother sooth the edge of my father's emotions too many times to believe it could disappear. But that was manageable. It could be worse. After a few, more volatile relationships in college, I knew I was better off staying away from this kind of guy.

He was my neighbor, and I knew nothing about him. Nothing. Maybe I couldn't stop the heat rising inside me each time Niklas came close enough to touch, but I could decide to stay away. And this also meant that I had to forget that his kiss on the stairs was the most delicious thing I had tasted in a long, long time.

Slowly, I walked back to my apartment door and let myself in. A walk in the park now felt out of the question. I wasn't ready for another run-in with Niklas, especially not after he had fled down the stairs so abruptly. The city still had hours to sleep. I looked down at the black camera bag in my hand for consolation. At least I had something to do now.

Closing the apartment door behind me, I walked down the hallway to the kitchen, the room farthest away from the front door. I wouldn't hear Niklas's footsteps or the creak of his door from here. I set the camera bag down on the table and unzipped it, carefully removing each of the lenses, lining them up on the table. Yes, this was a consolation, and a good one, too, I told myself. I'd worry about the entanglements of the trade—and what might follow—later.

8
"Who is that guy?"

The subway ride took me straight through the center of Stockholm with stops that Veronica had translated for me, *T-Centralen*, Central Station, and *Gamla Stan*, Old Town, places I had been meaning to visit all week long. But instead of getting off at one of these stations, I continued through the city until the subway reemerged from underground for a view of the enormous round building that rose up on the other side of the water. *Globen*, it was called, though it looked less like a globe and more like a giant golf ball.

As the large, white building came closer, I gripped Niklas's black camera bag, my body tingling with excitement. I would finally test the camera and lens for what it was supposed to be best at: clear, fast-action shots.

The intercom announcements on the train were completely unintelligible, and most of the stops had names that neared twenty letters long, so I kept my eyes fixed on the map and the signs closely. Finally, with a little audio jingle, a word I recognized popped up on the screen: *Globen*.

I exited and followed the flow of people heading toward what looked, close-up like some sort of white space station. On the left side of the doors, beyond the stream of fans, I could see Ludvig, waiting for me with a pass in his hand.

"Hello," he said, kissing me on the cheek. I smiled uncertainly. Did the kiss mean this was a date, or was this just the standard European way of greeting someone? Before I could come to any conclusions, we were pulled into the throng of fans pouring into the arena doors. Luckily, Ludvig seemed to know where we were going.

"We'll take the press entrance next time, but I wasn't sure you'd be able to find it."

Next time. We would be attending the games together, apparently.

He walked me back outside and then steered me around to another door, flashing our passes. We entered into a hallway and then turned down another one, underneath the bleachers, until we came to the rink-side opening. The cool air sent a shiver through me, and the smell of indoor ice and sweat took me back to Michigan, pushing through the crowds at Yost Arena.

But I wasn't back home. I was across the Atlantic, in Stockholm, waiting for the Swedish national team to skate out onto the ice. The arena hummed with energy. Finland was already circling around their end of the rink, evoking both jeers and cheers from behind me, some of them sounding surprisingly slurred for an afternoon game.

I had never been particularly interested in sports. It didn't help that my mother grew up on a dusty ranch, in a family where ideas like extracurricular sports were as foreign as deciduous trees. The second-rate status of the only sport my father ever loved, soccer, served as yet another reminder that he would forever live in a foreign country, no matter how many years he had been a US citizen. So aside from the incomprehensible chatter of Univision soccer on Saturdays, I managed to escape the draw of sporting events until college, despite growing up in a Big Ten state.

Even now, entering the hockey arena felt like entering a foreign culture, with its own dress codes, customs and ritual chants surrounding me. I'd probably find the crowd just as interesting as the game, though I knew enough not to take my eyes off the ice once the puck dropped. But right now, as the teams entered, I focused on the endless seats behind me: the rows of bare-chested men with faces painted white and blue, the colors of the Finnish flag; a long line of kids with matching jerseys—maybe a hockey team, coming to see their national idols in action; couples with matching t-shirts, blue and yellow, the letters SWE across the chest.

"What do you think?" Ludvig's voice startled me. In the midst of all the noise and excitement, I had forgotten he was standing so close.

"There are a lot of rowdy fans," I said, looking around. "I just hope the losing team doesn't take it too hard."

"The Sweden-Finland game is always a big rivalry. There should be a lot of good action, lots of emotion," he said, then pointed to my camera. "That's the perfect lens for a game like this."

"Thanks. It's—" I broke off, not sure what I wanted to say about my camera situation. "A friend and I switched for bit."

Though Niklas wasn't quite what I'd call a friend, I was at a loss for any other description. But Ludvig seemed to accept this explanation without giving it much thought.

"Who are you shooting for?" he asked.

I gave him the name of Connor's publication, and he smiled approvingly.

Connor had eventually written back saying he couldn't get me a pass for the games, but his department would probably buy a couple of good shots if I found a way in. It was no guarantee, but it was a start. In other words, I had no idea if my photos would actually be published, a reality that made me sound amateur at best. But that probably wasn't the kind of information I should be sharing with the guy who got me the rink-side spot. And I wasn't an amateur, I reminded myself. I had experience, just not in the sports world...another piece of information I probably shouldn't highlight for Ludvig.

"I love standing here next to the rink. I love these games," he said, looking straight into my eyes now, waiting for a nod of agreement.

I tilted my head to the side, trying to see this scene through his eyes.

"The energy from the crowd just feeds the players until they're like animals out there," he said. His voice was growing louder as he continued. "What's left is raw aggression. They're what we all are, without society to keep us in line. It's why everyone loves the fights. People pay to see these guys do what the rest of us aren't allowed to do. And if you and I get lucky, we'll capture a piece of that with our cameras."

I watched as Ludvig's face became more and more animated as he talked. I had a hard time imagining any raw aggression hidden behind the wiry, mild-mannered guy standing in front of me, but he spoke with the air of authority on the subject that made me wonder if everyone else besides me did, in fact, come here to witness aggression in its rawest form. Was I the only one who saw the intensity in sports photography as something different, not as a snapshot of the baser reality of human nature but as the exposure of a deeply private moment?

To me, capturing the rage of a fight was more like photographing the victims of a hurricane. The pictures were statements about the emotional intensity of that moment, not about the nature of those people themselves. But there was a fundamental difference between hurricane victims and athletes: Athletes were paid to play out these scenarios, with all the repercussions attached, all acknowledged from the beginning, under the watchful eyes of fans. I wondered if any of these ideas had already crossed the minds of the hockey players that were circling the ice in front of me.

Up until the start of the game, I wandered around, focusing the camera on the crowd, but when the puck dropped, I was pulled into the action. I was close enough to hear the players grunt and mutter as they passed by. It took a moment to channel back to my Michigan Daily assignments, but soon I was following the action, ready for something to happen.

It didn't take long. Just before the six-minute mark, two Finnish players broke away with only one Swedish player on their left in pursuit. Just as the Swedish player caught them, one of the Finnish players reached his stick out and tripped him. The second Finnish player shot ahead, curved around the goalposts and, at the last second, slid the puck in behind the goalie's skate.

The crowd erupted. I panned my camera back towards the middle of the ice, hoping to catch the moment of celebration, but instead what I found was a fight: The Swedish player had picked himself up off the ice and was now swinging at the Finnish player who had tripped him. His teammates rushed over to pull him back, but not before the Finnish player grabbed hold of his helmet, which tumbled down on the ice. The blood from his nose spilled onto his jersey. I took picture after picture, against my better judgment, as the Swede broke loose for another attack.

Then I drew in a sharp breath as I registered the scene in front of me. *Niklas.* The player out on the ice, the guy in blue and yellow swinging wildly at the Finnish player, despite the referee's repeated whistles, was Niklas. The same Niklas who had kissed me in the stairwell. Niklas, who had instinctively pushed away my camera when I had pointed it at him. Now, I had just captured his explosion on camera. His camera.

"You okay?" Ludvig's voice came from far away. "You look like you need to sit down."

I nodded.

Ludvig looked around for a chair. "You don't like the blood?"

I found myself nodding, not ready to explain what was really going through my mind. Finally, I asked, "Who is that guy?"

He furrowed his brow. "The Swedish player? Niklas Almquist. Former Red Wing. Quick player, great record but too much temper. Injured his knee earlier this season, then got suspended for violence off the rink. Someone leaked photos of it to the press. You've never heard of him?"

"No," I whispered.

"I don't follow hockey," I admitted, too dazed to care what he thought about that piece of information.

"Well, this is Sweden, and everyone knows our

country's best NHL players, so you should, too. We'll see how he reacts to questions about the fight tomorrow at the press conference, if he even shows up. He rarely says a word these days, but his English is excellent, and he's one of their stars, so they'll try to make him take some questions from the international press. You should be there. It's a good way to get to know the players and get a feel for the team."

A press conference? Niklas would be sitting on the other side of the table, looking out at the reporters and photographers. This could be what he tried hard to avoid. Was that why he had turned away at the café when the woman grabbed his arm? Was it that he didn't want to be recognized in public? It was possible. If this was true and I went to the press conference tomorrow, I would be right there with all the other members of the press, looking back at him. Though I barely knew him, I had a feeling that Niklas wouldn't react well when he saw me. In fact, I probably wouldn't either if I were him.

The fight was over, and Niklas and the Finnish player had skated off to the penalty boxes. The game was continuing without me. I couldn't think about Niklas right now. I was here to get some good, marketable photos. I could make decisions about Niklas later.

As the clock counted down the last minutes of the game, the score was tied, 2-2, and both teams looked tired from the increasingly rough checks that left the boards shaking. Finland took the puck down the ice for a last attempt on the Swedish goal. Niklas passed by, close enough to touch, to hear his breath. But at this moment it was clear that nothing else in the world mattered to him besides the Finnish player just ahead of him with the puck.

Niklas skated faster, closing in on the white jersey. With a final push, he was right behind the guy. Reaching forward, Niklas wove his stick between the Finnish player's stick and his skate without touching either. Then, with a little flick, he stalled the momentum of the puck long enough to pull it away. The Finnish player turned around and threw Niklas off balance, but not before Niklas passed the puck back to his teammate at center ice. With only seconds left, the Swedish player took off for the Finnish goal. The white jersey couldn't catch him—he was too far ahead.

The grunts of the Swedish player sounded as he charged the goalie. With less than two meters between them, the Swedish player moved left. The goalie followed him and, as the yellow jersey closed in on him, the goalie sank to his knees. He took a chance, throwing his weight to that same side. But his effort came a moment too soon. The Swedish player cut right at the last minute. Just before the yellow jersey glided past the goal post, he snuck the puck in. The buzzer rang. Sweden had scored the final goal, edging out Finland, 3-2.

I caught on camera the rush of the celebratory hugs

as the Swedish players gathered around Niklas and the forward that had scored the goal. Niklas's face was alive with a look I couldn't remember seeing in a long time. It was a look of true, uncomplicated happiness. The kind of happiness that the weights of adult life rarely allowed.

This must be why Niklas played. I lowered my camera and just watched him.

"What a game," yelled Ludvig. When I turned, I could see he had been just as swept away by the events of the last few minutes as everyone else.

"I could tell Sweden would win tonight. Almquist had that look on his face, like he's going to get whatever he wants, no matter what."

I swallowed, taking in Ludvig's last words.

He turned to me and tapped my camera. "Did you get the shots you wanted?"

"Um…" There wasn't any good answer to his question.

"You really need to be shooting the whole time if you don't want to miss the best moments. You can't just watch the game, waiting for something exciting to happen, and then lift your camera."

I rolled my eyes. Of course, I knew this, but it would be pointless to explain why my mind was far from photography right now. Ludvig was still talking to me, but I couldn't take my eyes from Niklas.

I felt Ludvig staring at me now. He must have asked me a question. I turned to him and was met with an intense gaze, making me wonder what, exactly, he imagined our relationship to be. Out of the corner of my eye, I could see the players begin to skate off the rink. It was time to leave. Ludvig started to escort me to the press doors and back out into the blinding sunlight.

"What did you say back in the arena?" I asked.

"Can I drive you home?"

He was already heading us away from the subway station, towards his car, I assumed. But the last thing I wanted was to be stuck in a car listening to Ludvig's photography tips.

So I shook my head and gently pulled my arm away.

Ludvig recovered almost immediately. "Then I'll meet you here tomorrow for the press conference?"

The idea gave me a cold, sinking feeling inside my stomach. I didn't want Niklas to see me there. And that was a terrible reason to say no to the career opportunity Ludvig was handing me.

"Yes, tomorrow," I said before I could change my mind. "And thanks for the press pass."

Then I turned back towards the subway station.

9
Another kiss from that sexy mouth

I sat at the kitchen table, laptop in front of me, eating a sandwich. Veronica had shown me a strange (and, apparently, traditionally Swedish) concoction: shrimp, hard-boiled eggs, mayonnaise, thinly-sliced cucumbers, dill and some sort of caviar paste from a tube, all on a slice of bread. Now I found myself oddly craving it. I took a bite of the picture-worthy arrangement and scanned my shots from the game one more time.

If these photos were going to be worth anything, I needed to send them out soon, but choosing which photos to send wasn't easy. By far, the photo that best captured the intensity of the game was the shot of Niklas, blood running from his nose, going for another swing at the Finnish player. But it was the photo I knew I wouldn't send out. Most likely, Connor would buy it, especially after hearing Ludvig's story about Niklas's previous fighting, both on and off the ice. Still I couldn't send it out, if for no other reason than the fact that it came from Niklas's own camera. Instead, I attached one last photo, Niklas's final steal of the puck, which had led to Sweden's game-winning goal. With a deep breath, I sent the message.

Now that the photos were out, my mind went straight to the press conference. Instinct told me I shouldn't go, but that same instinct made me frown. One game into this new turn in my career I was already backing out to save someone's feelings. Someone I hardly knew. Was I hesitating just because he kissed me? Before the events of the last few days, I wouldn't have guessed that I would be so willing to put aside such a clear advance in my career.

But this was no ordinary kiss. This was the kind I had read about in books I had hidden away as a teenager, the kind I never quite believed was real. And this kiss had been very real, real enough to push aside every other thought in my head. For those moments, I only *felt*—his soft, warm mouth, his tongue coaxing mine, the sensuous pull of his teeth against my bottom lip, his hands pressing me into the hard muscles of his body.

Still, I kept coming back to the man I had seen out on the ice. The man who had shown both startling violence and overwhelming joy during the game today. What did he do with those parts of him when there was no rink?

I glanced at the time. It was just before 5:00 pm. Filip was still at work, and Veronica was probably home. I stuffed the camera back in the bag and headed downstairs.

Veronica answered on the third knock, her clothes splattered with paint.

"Wait for me in the kitchen," she said, letting me through. "I'm just finishing up."

I wandered down the hallway and into the kitchen, taking in the design details. Veronica's influence definitely showed. I admired how she had managed to find the meeting point between the bright blues and patterns of Mexico and the preference for sleek lines and minimalist white in Swedish design. The counters were tiled in blue, and the color echoed in various corners of the room. The table and chairs were wooden and rustic, all painted white, and an elaborately stitched cloth from Mexico covered the table.

How did Veronica make this work? How could she live in a country so foreign from her own, far away from her family? As much as I loved to travel, I couldn't imagine being away forever.

I studied the long, white wall lined with Veronica's paintings. The images were at once both simple and elaborate. The bird against the starry night in front of me was quite simple and one-dimensional, but there were the colors upon colors of wavy lines running through the body and out into the tail feathers, each wave decorated with intricate patterns that made the painting come alive.

"Beautiful," I whispered when Veronica's footsteps

came from behind me.

"Thanks," said Veronica. I turned in time to see a rare blush on my friend's cheeks. "I think I finally found a dealer. I wasn't sure if I would be able to paint here in Sweden, but it turns out that just the opposite is true."

"Because you miss Mexico?"

"Maybe. But I never painted like this when I was in Mexico—or even at Michigan, either. There's something freeing about living so far from home."

Veronica had now traded her painting clothes for a simple black dress. She unclasped a colorful barrette and let her dark, wavy hair swing down over her shoulders as she headed for the kitchen counter. Veronica was still very much the same person that had walked into my dorm room on the first day of college, chattering with her mother in Spanish at a pace I couldn't hope to keep up with, and plopping herself down on the bed I had already claimed. But at the same time, as I watched my friend set up a plate full of cinnamon rolls and tiny cookies, I could see Veronica was at home here.

"What do you miss most?" I asked.

"Family, of course. The sun in the wintertime. Close friends. The few friends I have live all over Stockholm, so we don't see each other very often. We have dinner with some of Filip's friends a couple times a month, but the Swedish women I've met don't seem to be very interested in friendships, at least not the kind

I'm used to."

"That sounds like a lot of things to miss."

"It took a long time to adjust," said Veronica, her smile faltering a little. "But you haven't asked me what I got in return."

"Your paintings?"

"Yes, that, too." Veronica laughed. "But I have Filip. He is enough to keep me here, even if there were nothing else. And there's always been a part of me that was curious about whatever was just out of sight, and living abroad keeps that part of me satisfied. It's the reason I came to the University of Michigan while all my sisters stayed in my hometown. Going to college in a place that had snow was as different a life as I could think of at the time."

I considered my own future, which was far from clear. "I don't know. As much as I want to travel, I have a hard time imagining living this far away from home."

"Then you don't have anywhere near the imagination I thought you did, *Carolita*."

The combination of her sassy tone and my old nickname coming out of Veronica's mouth sent both of us into a fit of laughter.

"How was the game?" said Veronica, pouring us both cups of steaming espresso from the hot metal pot.

My smile dissolved. "That's what I came to show you."

I took out the camera and turned it on, scrolling through the photos.

"Nice camera," said Veronica. "Happy you accepted Ludvig's pass now?"

"I guess you could say that," I said, "but look at this photo."

I searched until I found Niklas's fight.

"I bet there are plenty of publications that will buy that one," said Veronica, glancing at the screen.

"Maybe. But look closely."

I zoomed in until Niklas's face was perfectly clear, blood and all.

"No…" said Veronica softly.

"Yes. And this is his camera."

Veronica studied the face on the screen.

"That look on his face—he looks like he's…," her voice trailed off, but I could fill in the rest of the sentence by myself. He looked like he was going to punch the next person that came near him, regardless of who it was. Like this was the last person you'd ever want to live across the hall from. Let alone kiss.

"I didn't submit the photo," I said. "I couldn't do it."

I filled Veronica in on what Ludvig had told me about Niklas's career and the photo scandal back in Detroit.

"I guess that explains his reaction to your camera. Though I still think it's a little extreme," said Veronica.

"I want to tell him that I was at the game and that I took some photos," I said, glancing back down at the image of Niklas on the camera screen.

"Why? He's a professional athlete. You didn't stalk him in order to take photos of him. This isn't his private life. It's his job."

But there was something uncomfortable about selling photos of Niklas when I hadn't told him first. It felt like I was somehow misleading him—at least if I were in his place, I would probably see it like that.

Veronica put her hand on mine and purposely exaggerated her Mexican accent. "You just want another kiss from that sexy mouth."

I couldn't help laughing again, but a rush of heat ran through me when I thought of kissing Niklas again. Veronica was right, at least partly so.

"How was I supposed to know he's a hockey player?" I said, still giggling. "He has all his teeth."

"Are you sure?" she asked, raising her eyebrows suggestively. "They could be fake. Research that the next time you kiss him and let me know."

"Sure. I'll get right on that," I said with a smirk.

"I haven't been out all day," said Veronica, brushing the crumbs from her hands. "Let's go for a long walk and find a new restaurant for dinner. Filip is working late."

A long walk sounded exactly like what I wanted to do.

"I just need to drop off the camera and change my shoes," I said, standing up. "I bought some new ones. My feet are killing me from all this walking."

Veronica smiled. "Welcome to Europe."

A few minutes later, I rubbed the blister forming on the back of my heel and slipped on my new tennis shoes. Then I grabbed my purse and locked the door.

I stopped. Footsteps in the stairwell. I stayed still, waiting for the person to wind around the narrow staircase into sight. Was it Niklas? My heart was thumping in my chest, though whether it was at the prospect of telling him about the photos or something else, I wasn't sure.

Niklas rounded the corner and stopped abruptly. He was clearly surprised to see me, and it didn't look like the good kind of surprise. It looked as if I were interrupting something, though I couldn't imagine what that something could be. Then I watched his eyes move from my dress to my tennis shoes, and the faintest hint of a smiled crossed his face. But the smile—if there ever was one—disappeared almost immediately. He nodded in my direction and then continued up the stairs, past me, eyes on the ground.

"Niklas?" I said quietly as he unlocked his door.

He shook his head, keeping his eyes straight ahead.

"Later," he grunted, not looking in my direction. "I can't right now."

"Niklas," I tried again. "I wanted to tell you—"

But before I could finish my sentence, he slammed the door and locked it behind him.

What the hell? My frustration surged as I saw how easily he could blow me off. For the third time—or fourth? I was losing count. He slammed the door on me, even as I was trying to talk to him. Was this the kind of arrogance that professional sports bred in a guy? It was embarrassing to think I had thought about kissing him only a few minutes before.

One thing was certain: Whatever hesitation I had about going to the press conference the next day was gone.

10
What was I trying to do? Hide?

The press conference room was smaller than I had imagined it would be. The front was lined with a long row of tables and microphones. Only a few feet away from those tables, rows of chairs had been set up for the media—which included me, I reminded myself.

Apart from the hockey federation banners that hung behind the players' seats, the rest of the room was white. We were there early, thanks to Ludvig, and only a few other photographers and writers were seated in the front row. Maybe I could think of a reason we should sit further back in the room. But what was I trying to do? Hide? I was here, and he was going to see me at some point. The idea of trying to avoid him sounded laughable, even childish, and it made the uneasiness inside of me worse.

Ludvig led me over to the second row of chairs. Niklas sure wouldn't miss me there, I thought, irritated with myself for still second-guessing my decision to come. Unless I was ready to run out now, it was much too late to change my mind.

"Do you want to move to the front?" Ludvig asked, leaning over and whispering in my ear as we sat down.

I shook my head.

His aftershave, noticeable at a distance, was overwhelming at close range. Again, I asked myself what this afternoon was to him—an extended favor? A date? The way he leaned into me suggested the latter, and I wasn't sure what to do with that idea. It wasn't that Ludvig was unattractive, I thought as I glanced over at him. His blond hair was again waxed into a careful mess in the front, hanging over a tanned face—surprisingly tanned, considering the fact that summers were rumored to be short and often cold in Sweden. In fact, he was quite good looking, and there was no reason I shouldn't feel attracted to him. Maybe attraction would grow if we spent more time together? He would certainly be a sensible choice.

So why was it Niklas I couldn't stop thinking about? Niklas, with his unpredictable moods and his scarred hands and the kisses that kept me awake long into the night. Niklas, who ignored me as I called after him like an idiot. Professional athletes had a reputation even I knew about—lots of sex with as many women as possible, women who never seemed to be in short supply, if I remembered correctly the entourages that followed the University of Michigan players around. Was this what Niklas would want from me?

I could feel the mix of anger and humiliation building. Maybe it was better that Niklas would see me here at the press conference. If I was just one in a long line of women Niklas kissed and then forgot about, it was a good thing we hadn't moved farther than that. I'd rather him think I was a photojournalist pursuing him for a good shot than a woman throwing myself at him in hopes for an encounter with the excitement and virility elite sports were supposed to produce.

More journalists filed through the door, filling up the seats and lining up along the sides, chattering in different languages. Ludvig had been talking to me for a while, something about the different brackets and the odds of Sweden facing the U.S. team. I should be paying attention. Connor had passed along my photos with this message: "Good start but faster turn-around, more action. This isn't the Michigan Daily anymore." I clearly didn't know how the world of professional sports photography worked, and Ludvig, in the seat next to me, wanted to explain it all. Right next to me was the door to the career break I had hoped for, the opportunity to earn enough money to hold me over while I traveled and built up a portfolio, but I was having a hard time mustering the enthusiasm for it.

The door opened again. Conversations stopped, and the press, almost exclusively male and, I guessed, mostly Swedish, began to clap. I turned and watched as the players along with another, older man—probably the coach—walked up behind the row of tables at the front of the room and sat down. Niklas was seated at the far end from me and was looking down the row at his teammates. He had on a dress shirt and tie, and his face seemed to have mostly recovered from the brawl. His smile was somehow different. In a word, he looked professional. Like a distant relative to the man I had seen yesterday on the ice.

As far as I could tell, he hadn't seen me yet. As Ludvig had predicted, they were starting with the Swedish portion of the press conference, so I tuned out the foreign melody of words around me and studied the players instead. I took the lens cap off and moved my camera down the line of men, trying not to stop too long at Niklas. This was difficult.

It was clear why the coach chose Niklas to speak, despite his reported reluctance to meet the press these days. He was engaging to watch. While the other players stumbled over their sentences or muttered one-word replies, Niklas looked at ease in front of the crowd. He made the press laugh more than once. In fact, this clean-shaven version of him looked more like someone in a boardroom meeting than on the hockey rink. Of course, it also helped that, unlike the guy sitting next to him, he wasn't missing any teeth.

I saw out of the corner of my eye that Ludvig was just as captivated by Niklas as I was. I looked back and forth between the two men. What did Ludvig see when he looked at Niklas? The same animated eyes and determined jaw I found myself staring at? Or did he just see the player that was on the ice yesterday. "The animal," as Ludvig had put it.

It also occurred to me that if Niklas hadn't spotted me yet, it was possible he'd leave the room without seeing me at all. At this point there were a lot of people packed into the little room, after all. Even that idea didn't give the kind of relief that I thought it would.

The press conference finally switched over to English, and I lowered my camera to listen. After a few questions for the coach, one of the journalists near me turned to Niklas.

"The Russian press sees Sweden as one of the tournament favorites," he began in what I guessed was a Russian accent, "as long as you can keep your temper under control. After the game against Finland, can you comment on this?"

When I looked back to Niklas for his response, I caught my breath. He was staring straight at me, not at the journalist a few seats down. The room was silent, waiting for his answer, but he continued to look at me with a mixture of surprise and something else on his face. Not quite anger, but something close.

Earlier that morning, I had prepared myself for the moment he saw me, yet I still was caught off guard. Immersed in the press conference around me, I had somehow begun to doubt that it would really happen.

Now he was staring at me across the room, and the calm, professional look was gone. Instead, his face was filled with emotion. This was the man I had gotten a glimpse of in my hallway. For a long, long moment, I just stared back, my gaze locked on his. Everyone else seemed to be staring at me as well, including Ludvig. It was too late to hide behind my camera or leave the room or do anything except meet the eyes that burned into me.

But the look on his face lasted only a moment. The Niklas I knew was gone as his gaze moved back to the man sitting just a few seats from me.

"I'll do whatever it takes for our team to win," Niklas answered and stood up, signaling that the press conference was over. The people surrounding me stood up, too, shouting questions and snapping photos as the team filed out, but I stayed seated, not wanting to see Niklas again. Nothing I had done to him was intentionally deceitful, but I felt the weight of his eyes on me. Betrayal. That was what I had seen on his face when he stared at me.

But he slammed the door in my face when I tried to tell him. I frowned, the thought of our encounter of yesterday only adding to my frustration.

"Do you know Almquist?"

Ludvig's voice interrupted my thoughts. I unclenched my hands from around Niklas's camera. I looked up at Ludvig and was met with yet another pair of accusing eyes.

"A little." I sighed. "He lives across the hall from where I'm staying, and he probably didn't expect to see me here. I didn't know he was a hockey player until the game yesterday."

Now it was Ludvig's turn to stare at me with a look I didn't bother trying to decipher. I had told him the truth, or at least all Ludvig needed to know of it, but the doubt on his face was clear. The rest of the room was emptying, leaving only the two of us to pack up our bags. But neither of us moved.

"I told you yesterday he's a brute," Ludvig snapped in a low voice. "Back when he was on the Red Wings, he got into a lot of trouble. Assault. Do yourself the favor of looking it up. It was all over the papers. You'd be smart to stay away from him."

I was silent. This was the first time I had seen a break in Ludvig's careful exterior, and I wasn't sure how to respond. It was difficult to reconcile the Niklas from my building, the man who had worried about my walking alone in the park and escorted me home, with a man who would assault someone, but I guessed that Ludvig wouldn't be interested in this line of conversation right now.

Ludvig didn't take his gaze from me. "Players like Niklas just think they can do whatever they want because they're famous and make lots of money." His voice was calmer now, but the edge of anger hadn't disappeared entirely.

I considered Ludvig's statement. I had the sinking feeling that this particular description did seem to fit the Niklas I knew, the one who slammed the door on me twice. I turned to look at Ludvig.

"Yesterday you said that players like Niklas show us our true nature, what we'd be without society. That they're paid to do what the rest of us aren't allowed to do. Were you talking about assault, too?"

Ludvig's eyes widened, and he stared at me a while.

"They're just animals," he finally said, not bothering to mask his contempt.

He stuffed the last of his equipment into his bag. As I stood up to do the same, he turned back around and put his hand on my arm. Ludvig's face was uncomfortably close to mine, and I suddenly wondered if he was going to try to kiss me. But he didn't. Instead, he spoke softly this time.

"Look, I'm sorry if I sound harsh. I don't think it's in people's nature to assault—that's not what I meant. I just don't want Niklas to do the same thing to you."

I gave him a half smile.

"I'm pretty good at looking after myself," I said, though Niklas had cast doubt on that idea.

But Ludvig nodded.

"How about going out for lunch?" he said. He searched in his bag and pulled out a neat stack of papers. "It's the schedule of the games. I've circled the higher-profile ones I think we should be at. We can plan at the restaurant."

I shook my head. "There's something I need to do."

Ludvig's face fell, and his expression tugged at me with a mixture of doubt and irritation. He had only invited me to a work-related lunch, one that I would professionally benefit from. Veronica would have told me this if she was standing there. In fact, it was this hypothetical conversation with Veronica that pushed me to add, "How about tomorrow instead?"

Ludvig's smile was back. "Great. I'll pick you up."

I took the hockey schedules that he was still holding out for me, but as soon as I looked up at his satisfied smile, I regretted letting those words out of my mouth.

11
The worst kind of stranger

Actually, what I had told Ludvig was not quite the truth. There was nothing I *had* to do. Only something I wanted to do. I wanted to know the story behind Niklas's assault, and I knew the idea wouldn't leave me alone until I found out.

I stared through the subway window as it crossed the bridge to Stockholm, only to dive back underground into the city. After a few more stops, the train emerged again, giving me a view of Old Town, surrounded by water. Yellow and orange buildings lined the waterfront, all with copper roofs, turning green from the elements. They were packed neatly onto the little island that peaked in spires and towers in the distance.

As the train sped underground again, my thoughts wandered back to the press conference and to Ludvig's face as we spoke in the empty room. For a moment even-tempered Ludvig had looked furious, both with

Niklas for the assault and with me for having a connection to him. I found Ludvig's reaction just as surprising as the idea of Niklas's assault. His contempt for Niklas had been tinged with something else, something I, distracted by Niklas, couldn't quite identify at the time. I closed my eyes, trying to replay Ludvig's words back at the rink and inside the press conference room. Was it envy? I opened my eyes again and looked out the window, into the darkness of the subway tunnel. Could Ludvig, so polished and controlled, be jealous of Niklas? When we had first met in Veronica's apartment, Ludvig himself had mentioned he wanted to play hockey at one point. The idea of him out on the rink was hard to imagine.

The recording of a soothing woman's voice came over the intercom and made an announcement in Swedish I was beginning to recognize: St. Eriksplan, the name of my station. I walked quickly out of the station and through the streets, back into the dark, cool hallway of the apartment building, hesitating for a moment at the top of the stairs. Niklas's door was dark and solid, completely unchanged from the dozens of times I had passed by, and yet I stared at it, as if looking for a signal. Nothing happened.

Why was I still inexplicably drawn to him? Was he drawn to me as well? It had felt that way, but there was something else there, too. With a sigh of exasperation, mostly directed at myself, I opened my own door and walked in.

Finally, the place was beginning to feel familiar, almost like my own. I entered the kitchen and opened the refrigerator. There wasn't much to choose from, just various sandwich fixings that I had been experimenting with. I pulled out a few items and assembled a simple arrangement: opened-faced on buttered brown bread, with cheese and two slices of tomatoes. Then I walked over to the kitchen table, where my laptop waited for me. No more stalling. It was time.

But now that I had a chance to look up Niklas's history, I hesitated. Did I really want to get the story from the press first? Nothing about the man I had met in person—the man who had steered his friend away from me in the park, who had walked me home, who had kissed me so tenderly and thoroughly—matched someone who would assault a person. I wanted to hear the story from him. That is, if I could get him to talk to me without slamming the door.

I shook my head. Was I really still waiting for this guy? I took a deep breath and typed in the search words: *Niklas Almquist News.* But before I could press Enter, I heard a knock on the front door. I was halfway down the hall when the second knock came, more urgent than the last. I peered through the peek hole. Niklas was standing impatiently close to the door. My heart gave a hard jolt. I swallowed hard and opened it.

"Niklas." I gulped. Despite all my apprehensions over the last day, at that moment, as he stood in front of me, all I could think about was how much I wanted him. He had changed since the press conference and was now wearing jeans and a t-shirt that stretched across the muscles of his chest and showed his long, fit arms. His shaggy blond hair was under more control than usual, though one wavy lock threatened to fall down on his forehead. The cut on his brow was mostly healed, and his sky-blue eyes were looking right at me. Into me. And he had that same, brutal look on his face that he had given me earlier at the press conference.

"Your camera. I got it fixed." he said, handing it to me. I hadn't even noticed he was holding it.

"Thanks," I said, the flush creeping up my neck. The camera, of course. That's why he had come over. And he wanted his own back. "Come in. I'll get yours."

His expression changed a little, and he hesitated before stepping through the doorway.

"You shouldn't let strange men into your apartment," he said in a low voice that was gentler than I had expected.

"And that's you?" I said with a smirk.

But he didn't smile. "I'm the worst kind of stranger. The kind people think they know."

My mind played with the possible meanings behind his statement. Ludvig's warning came back to me. Should I be scared of this man? Nothing in my experience with him felt dangerous, but Niklas himself had pointed out just how unattuned I was to danger a few days before. Still, the tension between us felt like something much different.

"Just come in," I finally said.

He drew in a sharp breath when his body brushed against mine. I felt it too, and it was enough to awaken the physical memory of our kiss. The apartment was so quiet as we walked down the hall, just our footsteps and the sound of his low breath behind me. As I started to turn into the kitchen to grab his camera bag, I caught sight of my laptop. It was on the table where I had left it, open, with my search words clearly typed into the box. Pictures of him, mostly in his Red Wings jersey, spread across the screen.

Shit. I caught my breath and then turned around, finding Niklas only inches away from me. My heart gave a sudden jump, though I wasn't sure if it was nervousness or the tension that sparked every time we were near each other. The heat from his body flooded through me, and I had to consciously stop myself from reaching out and touching him.

"Sorry," he said gruffly. He took a step back and looked away.

My mind was having trouble working, but I managed to point across the hall and say, "You can go into the living room. I'll find it."

He nodded and moved past me, but not before glancing into the kitchen. Did he see what was on my screen? If he did, he didn't let it show on his face. He simply turned and walked into the other room.

I let out my breath slowly. I slipped into the kitchen, closed the laptop and grabbed the camera bag off the table. I found Niklas pacing at the other end of the living room. When he heard me enter, he crossed back over in long strides, ignoring the bag in my hand. He stopped in front of me but seemed unsure of what to do next. He ran his hand through his hair and then looked down at me.

"Why didn't you tell me you'd be at the press conference?" His words were slow and controlled, and his gaze bore into me.

"I didn't know who you were before I went to the game yesterday. I had no idea you'd be there."

"I find that hard to believe."

My own frustration was building. "You're so well known that you find it hard to believe I didn't know who you are? That's quite an ego you have."

Niklas scowled. "I find it hard to believe that a sports photographer who came all the way from Detroit for a hockey tournament wouldn't know the players she was watching."

"But I'm not a sports photographer. At least I wasn't until yesterday," I said, trying to steady my voice. He was standing only a few inches from me, his hands clenched, and I could feel the heat of the tension in his body. But behind the tone of our conversation, I still felt the undeniable crackle of pure physical attraction. I steadied my voice and pushed on.

"I came here on a magazine job about ex-pats around the world. These hockey photos are just a last-minute way to fund my trip, a connection through my friend downstairs." I paused for a moment to get my breath and then added, "Besides, you weren't exactly straightforward with me. When I told you I was from Detroit, you didn't tell me you just moved from there."

"I…I have a bad reputation in Detroit. Really bad. But you probably know that by now." He was quiet for a moment as he let his words set in. When he spoke again, his voice was low and sad. "You made me laugh that night, breaking into your own apartment. It was the first time I'd really laughed in a long time. And then, in the hall—" Niklas paused, seeming to struggle with what to say next. Then he looked straight at me with his sky-blue eyes.

"Whatever happened between us, I just wanted it to have nothing to do with my past. I'm trying so hard to get out of that world, and I thought—" He stopped again. He shook his head, looking back at the floor.

The sound of our breaths filled the room, and the tension between us was growing stronger.

"What did you read about me in your search?" he asked quietly. So he had seen the computer screen when he had walked in. He sounded resigned.

"I didn't look yet," I whispered. "What will I find?"

"Bad things," he said. "Really bad."

Niklas looked so serious right now, and I had absolutely no idea where this was going. There was a part of me that felt untethered, as if the path in front of me had suddenly disappeared. Or maybe some part of me knew where this would lead; I just didn't want to look. I took a deep breath and asked my next question, though I wasn't sure if I was ready for the answer.

"Are these things true?"

"Some of them are," he said with a tight smile. "There were a couple times when I took things too far on the ice. But the worst things the papers say—those things aren't true, at least not the way they write them."

I nodded slowly, wondering what those really bad things could be. Did I want to know, even after he had said they weren't true? But before I could decide whether or not to ask, he began to talk again.

"When I'm on the ice, I'm not thinking anymore. The game's too quick for that," he said, his eyes still steady on mine. "I'm just acting and reacting. The danger for me, for anyone who spends his life training for a game like this, is that you can't live the rest of your life like that. In fact, it can get you into a lot of trouble if you're not careful. We all have ways of dealing with it, and some do better than others."

What was he trying to tell me? I had the feeling again that I was blindly stepping forward, but I couldn't stop myself.

"I deal with this by staying away from women that I think might get me—"

He stopped and looked at the ground, as if he were struggling with what to say next, as my insides sank. Get him...what? It sounded ominous. Niklas seemed to sense that the conversation was heading in the wrong direction, too.

"No, wait. Please listen," he said, and he lifted his hand to my cheek, coaxing me to look at him. "Caroline, everything about this is different. And I'm trying my hardest to figure out what to do about it. I want so much to have something with you, something more, something that's far away from hockey. But I need to be careful."

Oh.

The fact that I had met Niklas only a handful of times didn't seem to matter. The truth was that I had felt this same pull between us since the first morning we had met. I didn't know what to say. All I knew was that the rough brush of his hand on my cheek had the same effect as it had every time he touched me. I was taking short breaths, trying to concentrate on what he was saying, trying to contain all the things my body urged me to do.

"Part of me wants to warn you to stay away from me," he said quietly, "but the other part, well…"

His fingers stroked my cheek again and then his palm moved to my neck. He seemed to be waiting for me to take the next step. I looked up at him, so tender and serious. The lock of his hair that had caught my eye earlier had now fallen onto his forehead, and I brushed it away. And in that moment, I had made my decision— for now, at least.

"This has nothing to do with hockey," I whispered. "It didn't before, and it doesn't now."

Gently, I urged his head down to mine, and he obliged me, parting his lips and giving me another taste of his warm mouth. I could feel the smoldering heat from his body, and, yet, he still held back. I kissed him, and slowly his body came alive. He began to explore, tasting me. His lips were soft, but there was a roughness in his kiss, a hunger he seemed to be trying to keep hold of.

But when my hands began to trace a slow path down, over the flat, hard muscles of his chest and the ripples of his stomach, this ignited something in him. A low growl came from deep inside his chest as his mouth devoured mine. There was nothing gentle about his kiss anymore. Each swipe of his tongue, each caress of his lips held raw desire. Everything else around us disappeared except the sensations where our bodies met. His hands traveled along my sides, exploring the curve of my hips and stomach. Then he found my breasts, and I felt the deep jolt of pleasure as his fingertips circled and squeezed.

"*Oh*," I moaned, and I felt him react.

He stopped suddenly, as he did before in the stairwell. He groaned again as he pulled himself away and rested his arm on the wall over me, his large body heaving. This time I didn't let go of him.

"No," I said, my voice husky and breathless. "Please don't stop."

"Are you sure you want this?" His voice was low and ragged in my ear. "Because I don't want to hold back if we go any further."

"Yes, I'm sure," I whispered back as I lifted his shirt, running my hands up the trembling muscles of his stomach and chest. His skin was searing hot.

I pulled off his shirt, and then, as he hung over me, I slowly lifted my dress over my head, dropping it on the floor. I heard his camera bag drop, too. As my lips met his again, his hand moved up my thigh as I pressed myself closer to him.

Niklas pulled away again, but this time it was to lift me, and he did it with surprising ease. He carried me down the hallway and into the bedroom.

I buried my face in his neck and breathed in his scent, so enticingly male. I sighed. This was really happening. "Is this what you had in mind when you knocked on my door?"

"Not exactly," he said with a searing smile, "though I can't deny I've fantasized about it. More than once."

He set me down on the bed in front of him. My hands were not quite steady when I reached up slowly and unbuttoned his jeans. I slid them down, following his long, hard thighs and well-defined calves with my hands until I reached his feet. There was no denying he was built like an athlete, every part of him. His muscles tensed at my touch, and I heard him draw in his breath as I slowly ran my hands back up to his erection, throbbing and pulsing. Another low sound escaped his mouth as he lay me back onto the bed, hovering over me.

"Å, vad jag vill ha dig," Niklas whispered in my ear.

Then he began to kiss me all over, on my shoulders, on my neck, and then lower, onto the sensitive peaks of my breasts. Slowly, he made his way down my body in a trail of kisses. Then he spread my legs and kissed me again.

He was so much gentler and slower than I imagined he would be. I could feel the power behind his long, muscular body, but he took his time, and he seemed to be as lost in this experience as I was. His unhurried mouth explored every part of me, places I didn't even know I wanted to be touched. He licked and sucked until my own cries were muffled by the heavy thudding of my heart. And then he sucked a little harder, pushing me over the edge in waves of pleasure. I cried out.

He hovered over me, resting on his elbows as the last waves of pleasure echoed through my body. He kissed my neck and forehead, still slow and gentle despite the erection that was rock-hard against me.

"Do I want to know how you learned to do that so well?" I whispered.

Niklas's laugh was a low rumble. "Probably not."

I laughed, too, trying not to let my thoughts wander further in that direction.

"But I'd like to think I have a few more skills, too," he said, his smile getting broader.

"I bet you do."

He stroked my breast, his fingers sending flutters of pleasure through me. I couldn't believe that my body could respond so soon. But there were plenty of things about this evening that were hard to believe.

"Are you...?" his voice was tight with restraint now. "Do you want...?"

"I want you," I said, arching up to drag my teeth over his bottom lip. "Please. Now."

He didn't need any more prompting than that. With one hand under me, raising my hips to meet his, Niklas slowly entered. He closed his eyes and rested his forehead on mine, pushing deeper. A little cry escaped from my mouth, and he froze.

"Am I hurting you?"

"No," I gasped. "Don't stop."

I moved under him, my body trembling with renewed pleasure. I was impossibly full, but he kept moving deeper, adjusting, sliding in further. Finally, he stilled, his breath coming in short pants.

"Still okay?" he whispered in my ear.

I nodded, unable to speak. The sensation was overwhelming, and my body struggled to accommodate his size. Finally, my breath returned.

Then he began to move again in long, deliberate strokes. His gaze was hot and intense, and his face was filled with building pleasure. The dust of hair over the smooth, hard muscles of his chest skimmed my nipples as he lifted my hips for thrust after thrust. I wanted more, faster, harder and I held on tight as he gave it to me. My release came in long, racking spasms, and Niklas's low cries followed.

He held me tightly until the aftershocks eased. He kissed me over and over, on my lips, in my hair, and in the most tender places of my throat. Gently, he rolled to the side, keeping my body tight against his.

I was having trouble forming thoughts. It wasn't just the pleasure. The whole experience was much more intense, much more intimate than I expected. Nothing in my life had prepared me for anything like this. Of course, Brad and I had dutifully had sex on Saturday nights, and sometimes it was good. But sex with Niklas was something much, much different than fun.

*

"Why wouldn't you speak to me in the stairway after the game?" I asked. "I was trying to tell you I was there, too."

I lay on my back, my hair a tangled mess on the pillow. Niklas was on his side, his hand exploring the curve of my waist.

"I said, 'later,'" he said, raising his eyebrows. "I couldn't talk. It's more than I'd do for anyone else."

"And I'm supposed to be grateful for that?" I laughed. "*Ahh, the famous Niklas Almquist talked to me.*"

"That's not what I meant," he said, squeezing my thigh in its most ticklish spot and sending me into a fit of laughter. "I meant that I was trying."

Then his smile faded a little, and he pulled me closer to him. "Actually, I did want to talk to you. Badly. Or maybe a little more than talk," he said with a chuckle. "But not after a game. Not when I was—"

I studied his face, waiting for him to continue. He was looking out the window now. There was a wrinkle of seriousness between his eyes, and the corners of his mouth pulled tight. His large, warm hand had stopped at my shoulder.

Finally, he said, "This might not make a lot of sense right now, but I didn't want you to see that part of me. How I get when I play. I told you before that I have to be careful when I'm like that. When we walked together that morning out in Vasaparken, I felt like it was just you and me, not just the hockey player but the rest of me. And it felt so good, so easy. It's been a long time since I've felt like that with someone, and I didn't want to screw that up. I still don't."

I gave him a wry smile. "So you didn't want me to know you played hockey, but you were angry when you thought I deliberately kept my photography job from you?"

Niklas laughed.

"Okay, that's fair," he said. His fingers had dropped down from my shoulders and were now teasing my nipples. "But hockey brings out something in me, something I can't always control."

I was having a hard time concentrating on the conversation, but I had more questions for him. I tried

125

to remember what they were.

"What happens after this tournament? Do you go back to Detroit?"

He shook his head. "No. My contract wasn't renewed. I didn't play much this season because of injuries, and then there was—"

Again, he cut off his sentence. The alleged assault? But he had said that the worst wasn't true. His hand stopped its explorations, and a flash of anger crossed his face. As much as I wanted to ask what had happened, I could clearly see he didn't want to talk about it. I decided not to push the subject—not now.

"I just found out I wasn't going back not too long ago," he finally said.

And immediately, I was sure I knew exactly when he had found out. It was the night shortly after I had arrived, the night I had heard him through the walls.

"Djurgården offered me a contract," he said, adding, "That's the Stockholm team I played for before I went to Detroit."

I let my hand run along the side of his face. "Is that what you want?"

"What I want is to figure out what comes next. I've spent most of my life training for hockey, training to be quicker and stronger and more ruthless. To intimidate. To be single-minded. But there's not much I can do with that kind of training off the ice. Not much that won't get me arrested," he said with a bitter smile.

"I can think of a place for some of those skills." I

let my hand run across his chest and along the muscles of his arms. "Not all, but some."

Niklas laughed, and his expression relaxed. It felt so good to lie there with him, too good to think about all the reasons why I probably shouldn't be doing this. I tried to block out those thoughts, and his renewed explorations made that easier.

"Is this what you were thinking?" he said, his voice low and husky as he took my breast in his mouth. "I hope you're appreciating my single-mindedness."

"Definitely."

12
I know what you want

I wasn't sure how much actual sleep I got, if any at all. With the perpetual twilight of the Nordic summer night, I faded in and out of consciousness, somewhere between fantasy and reality. Niklas's body, so new next to mine, awoke something inside my own, and I didn't want to miss a moment of it, despite my exhaustion. He, too, stayed half awake, his hand over my hips as he lay behind me.

Sometime during the night, Niklas had gotten up to open the windows, letting in the cool nighttime air. He stopped at the low table at the foot of the bed and picked up one of the photographs.

"Are these yours?" he asked.

I nodded. "It's Mexico. We visited my father's home town when I was fourteen."

Niklas picked up each one and held it in his palm, studying it with interest. When he came to the last one, the back of the frame fell off, and he was left with the bare photo of my father's grief in his hand. He looked at it for a long time.

"Why is this one hidden?" he finally asked.

"I don't know," I said truthfully. "I guess it feels private. I don't want to see it every day, but I want it with me."

"Is it okay that I'm looking at it now?"

I nodded.

He was silent for a while again, just staring at the photo. Then he said, "Your parents really love each other, don't they."

It was a statement, not a question, it seemed. In all the years of holding onto that photo, I had never seen it in those terms. I had only seen my father's sacrifice, the pain and frustration that the distance from his family had caused him. But Niklas had found something different.

I crawled down the bed and sat next to Niklas, taking the photo from his hand. He was right. Their love for each other was there, just as much as my father's pain, if not more. I just hadn't looked for it before.

"Yes," I finally said, putting the photo back into his palm. "Yes, they love each other. Each gave up a lot to be together, but I don't know if either of them thinks about it that way."

I looked up at Niklas's face, trying to decipher his expression. He was watching me as if he were trying to answer some question of his own.

"What about your parents?" I asked.

He shook his head. "Not quite as rosy." The corners of his mouth pulled down. "Some other time I'll tell you. Not tonight."

He pulled me on top of him, and I settled into the warmth of his arms wrapped around my body, drawing me closer, his warm, hard muscles against mine. I rested my head on his chest. I must have drifted off for a moment but was woken up soon afterward by his clear arousal. I shifted, and he let out a hiss.

"I can't get enough of you, Caroline," he said into my ear with a wry laugh.

"I didn't know exactly what to expect from you," I said. "I guess I thought you'd be a little... rougher."

His eyes widen a little, and he took a while to respond. "If that's what you want, I'm more than willing to accommodate you," he said slowly.

"I'm not sure if that's what I want," I said. "I didn't know any of this was an option until tonight."

He closed his eyes at my words and took a deep breath. "I should let you sleep."

But I could feel his powerful urgency, and it awoke that same want in my own body.

"There are things I like better than sleep," I whispered.

A moment later, I was on my back with Niklas's body, hard and ready, on top of my own. He rolled on another condom, then took both my hands and lifted them over my head, holding them easily in one of his. A flash of the scene at the park, with him holding my hands together, pressing me against his body, rushed through me. He paused, checking for signs of doubt, but doubt was the last thing on my mind. Then he began. I cried out as he entered me with long, rough thrusts that took me to the edge almost immediately. How could my body react so intensely to his? He seemed just as lost as I was as his hips met mine, over and over, until I came again.

Minutes passed. Both dreamy and sluggish, he pulled me in close, and I drifted in and out, listening to the sound of his slow, steady breath in my ear.

I must have fallen into a deep sleep because the next time I opened my eyes, I found him sitting on the edge of the bed, looking back at me. I thought I would have awoken with his movement, but somehow, he had gotten up without me noticing. Now his hand smoothed my hair from my face and traced it down over my shoulder.

"I was supposed to be home hours ago. About nine hours ago, in fact," he whispered.

I looked at the clock on my nightstand. 6:00 am. The night was already over.

"What do you mean?"

"Curfew. I'm supposed to be in bed by 9:00 pm, and I don't think this is what my coach had in mind," he said, his lips curving into a smile.

I propped myself up on my elbows. Was he leaving, just like that?

"How many times have you used that line before?" I said it with a wry smile, but I could hear the edge in my voice.

"That wasn't very fair," he said softly.

He was right. But at the mention of hockey, I suddenly felt the imbalance of the situation. He had ignored me in the hall, came when he wanted and left when he was ready. And what was I supposed to do? Just wait to see if he decided to come back? There were so many reasons why I didn't want to be in this position. It reeked of more than one relationship in college that had left me feeling used, and those relationships didn't include sex. With those guys I hadn't felt anything near what I felt right now for Niklas.

"Then how does this work?" I asked, trying to soften my voice.

Niklas lay back down close to me and let his hand rest on my stomach.

"I don't know how this works," he said. He slid his hand up so that he held my cheek, his thumb tracing my bottom lip. "What would you like? You haven't told me anything about that."

That wasn't the answer I had expected. I opened my mouth but then closed it again. I had no idea what I wanted. What could I ask for? This apartment was mine for the month, and part of that month was already gone. Soon I would leave everything in Stockholm behind, including him. But at this moment, I wanted to bury myself in his touch and feel the length of his body on mine, over and over. Would the electric attraction between us run its course by the end of my time in Stockholm, or would it become something much harder to break away from? Even if he gave me the freedom to choose the course of the next few weeks—and that was a selfish assumption—I didn't know what to ask for.

"I don't know what I want," I finally said. "I'm not here forever."

The sharp edge in my voice was gone now. I ran my hand through his hair, down his neck and over the slope of his shoulder. Niklas closed his eyes, and I felt each of his muscles respond to my touch.

When he opened his eyes again, they were dark and heavy with desire. He leaned forward, and his kiss was long and slow.

"I can help you decide..." he whispered.

He had meant it as a joke, but there was an undercurrent of truth to his statement. There was nothing tentative about his advance now, and the kisses that followed were more direct than his words. *I know what you want*, they seemed to tell me, though these might have been my own hopes speaking.

I was surprised at how quickly he moved, despite his size. His muscles came alive as he reached for me. Before I knew it, I was on my back again, and he was on top of me. His hand gently brushed the hair out of my face and then found my breast. His touch sent a wave of pleasure through me that hadn't lessened, even after the night together. If anything, the feeling had grown stronger.

And he was ready for me as well; that much was clear. He was hard, and his breath was harsh and uneven. He moved his hand over the curves of my body, leaving a trail of heat in its path.

"God, how can I still want you so badly right now?" he growled. My answer was a gasp, *yes, yes*. I wanted him just as badly.

He lifted my hips and slowly entered me, and I moaned in pleasure. I met his eyes and beyond all the passion and lust, I saw something new there: happiness.

*

"I can't see you until the next match is over, until I've had a day to recover," he said, and he smiled apologetically. His jeans were on, but his chest was still bare and hot under my hands. "We should win this next one. It's against Switzerland."

I nodded, trying to ignore the powerful urge to press my body against his again. His voice was distant now when he talked about hockey, and I could feel the same uncertainty bubble up again. But then he smoothed back the mess of my hair and looked down into my eyes.

"But right now, I don't care. For the first time in as long as I can remember, I don't care about the game. I know I will again when I walk into practice today, but right now—" He stopped speaking and shook his head. "I have to go."

I watched as he slipped his t-shirt back on and grabbed his camera bag. Then I followed him to the door. His hands slid over my shoulders and down my arms, finding their way underneath the t-shirt I had slipped on.

"I'm sorry," he mumbled.

His hands were so warm against my skin. He found my lips and kissed them, softly at first and then with an intensity that threatened to reopen the desire that had kept me up all night. I broke it off.

"You'd better go, while I'm still standing," I said. I smiled, letting my hand rest on his arm once more before he disappeared out the door.

I sank into the chair next to the entrance. The warmth of his touch and the pressure of his hands were still on my skin. I closed my eyes, letting the remains of the night fill me before the intensity faded. I ached in places I didn't know I could ache. But the longer I sat there, the more exhaustion weighed down inside me, and with it came its usual companions: doubt and pessimism.

How did I end up like this again, nodding in agreement to someone else's plan, a plan that I really didn't like at all? Just because I couldn't make up my mind about what I really wanted. I meant to leave that behind when I left Brad, only to find myself right back where I started. Though it was true that he had asked me what I had wanted, what would he have said if I asked him to stay? I already knew the answer.

Is this what it would be like to be with Niklas: occasional nights of intense pleasure, followed by long periods without seeing him? I couldn't deny that being with Niklas was powerful. I didn't know that so much sex in one night was even possible, let alone the kinds of volatile emotions the experience had been laced with. But if right now was a glimpse into what the next few weeks with him would be like, I wasn't sure how I felt about it.

My stomach gave a loud growl, and I opened my eyes. Niklas had ordered food the night before, but I had been too distracted to eat much. And now I was starving. I walked down the hall to the kitchen, but when I turned the corner, I stopped. What I saw made all thoughts of hunger disappear. My camera bag was still sitting on the table, and I had given Niklas's camera back. Before I had taken back my memory card. With the photos of Niklas on it.

13
The European football championships...
in Spain

I was almost sure my alarm rang immediately after I lay down, though the clock suggested otherwise. And the few hours of sleep I had snuck in that morning seemed to have made me more drowsy, not less. I rubbed my eyes and looked at the clock again. No, I wasn't mistaken; it was 11:00 am. Ludvig would pick me up in thirty minutes. Sighing, I rolled out of bed and headed for the shower.

I had just slipped on a dress and was drying my hair with a towel when I heard a knock on the front door. I glanced at the clock. 11:15 am. What was he doing here so early?

"Just a minute," I called, quickly running a brush through the tangle of dark waves that dripped down my back. I headed for the door.

"Sorry. I wasn't expecting—"

I stopped mid-sentence when I looked up. It was

Niklas, standing once again outside my door and looking even more tired than I felt. And once again, he was holding a camera bag in his hand. The grim line of his mouth made me swallow a couple times before I spoke.

"The pictures of you," I said softly.

"What did you do with them?" His voice had a tight calm to it that made me feel worse. But why should I feel bad? Photographing his game was my job. Did he want me to apologize for catching him on camera, just like the rest of the photographers that lined the rink did? Personal photos were one thing, but photos of a game that he was paid to play, that people paid to see?

"I did the same thing that all the other photographers did with the photos they were paid to take," I said, my own voice taking on a tone much calmer than I felt. "I sent some of them to the news desk."

I was too annoyed to say that I had kept most of the photos of Niklas for myself. I wasn't ready to tell him that I had kept them not because of their worth on the news market but because instinct told me they were the part of him that he tried so hard to keep from me.

Instead, I said, "This is my career that I'm trying to build. And I already told you I didn't know you would be there. It was a job opportunity, and I took it. I also realize some of the photos aren't that flattering, but you were doing your job, and I was doing mine. Or is mine lower priority?"

My voice was not quite as even now. And when he answered, Niklas also sounded considerably less controlled.

"That's not what I'm saying at all," he said, his teeth clenched. "I'm saying you have a conflict of interest. Is our relationship personal or is it professional? Because I can't have it both ways."

"You're going to—"

My words were cut off by the sound of my intercom.

"It's Ludvig," he said when I pushed the button.

I buzzed him in and then looked back at Niklas. His blue eyes were icy.

"Should I leave before your date gets here?"

Was that...jealousy I heard in his voice?

"That was low, Niklas," I said, closing my eyes. "There's no date. We're covering another game."

I took a deep breath. We only had a minute before Ludvig would be at the door. I decided to just tell him the truth. "Niklas, I kept those pictures of you because they're of you, not because I was planning to sell them, okay? Because of the way you lent me your camera and kissed me in the hall. Not to publish, no other reason."

His jaw softened as he took in my words. I reached out and ran my fingers down the thick muscles of his forearm until I found the top of his hand. He didn't respond, but he didn't pull away, either.

"You can't...I don't want you to go to the

Switzerland game," he whispered.

I looked up at him, but before I could answer, Ludvig's knock came from the door. I let go of Niklas and opened the door.

"Hello, Caroline," said Ludvig and handed me a small pot of orchids. "A housewarming gift."

"Um, thanks," I said, turning red. "They're lovely."

Ludvig moved a little closer. "I thought you'd like something to make your apartment—"

Ludvig took a step forward, but his voice stopped. His mouth hung half way open, midway through his next word. Clearly, he had forgotten whatever he was going to say. Instead, he was looking up at Niklas, who had come into sight as he entered through the doorway.

Niklas's face was blank now, an inscrutable mask. It was not unlike the look I had seen on him at the press conference, but there was no trace of friendliness this time. And there was something about the way he was sizing up Ludvig that made Ludvig squirm.

I set down my new plant.

"Don't worry. I'll leave you two alone," said Niklas with a hint of sarcasm I decided to ignore.

"Niklas, this is Ludvig. Ludvig, Niklas—"

"—Almquist, Detroit Red Wing," Ludvig finished.

His eyes were wide in the sort of admiration that I imagined would grate on Niklas. After all that condescending talk about hockey players, Ludvig was clearly star-struck. I would have laughed if the mood was a little less tense.

Niklas raised his eyebrows and muttered, "*Former Red Wing.*"

He pushed past Ludvig and walked out the door.

I closed my eyes and let out my breath. When I opened them again, Ludvig was staring at me. He shook his head.

"You shouldn't have let him into your apartment."

This time I did laugh aloud. "It looked like you were happy to see him here just a few minutes ago."

He frowned. "Not with you. Not while you're alone."

I looked at the man standing in front of me. With his lanky frame and carefully styled hair, I couldn't imagine him trying to defend himself physically. If Niklas was a threat to me, he was as much of one to Ludvig, or just about anyone else I knew, for that matter.

It was useless to explain to Ludvig that Niklas had, in fact, spent the entire night in my apartment, and the tone was hardly threatening. Instead, I had found the kind of pleasure in one night with Niklas that had eluded me in all the years I had been with Brad. Everything about Niklas was unexpected and overwhelming. Late into the night, it was as if he had reached inside and found a connection that wouldn't let go. But none of this was a part of the world Ludvig existed in—and, I reminded myself, the world that Niklas was a part of as well.

Ludvig was still staring at me, waiting, I guessed,

for some sort of explanation of my relationship with Niklas. I wasn't going to give it to him.

"Let me get my things," I said, and I walked back into the kitchen to grab my camera bag.

*

Ludvig pulled into the parking lot at the bottom of a tower in the middle of an enormous grassy park, mostly deserted. From a distance, through the clumps of trees, the building looked communist-era stark and bunker-like, but when we walked in, the inside was surprisingly modern. We took the elevator to the restaurant near the top of the building. As I walked out into the room lined with long panes of glass, I stopped. The whole city stretched out in front of us. Mazes of roads, buildings, trees and waterways wove in and out of each other, spreading out in greens, blues and grays as far as I could see. Clouds hung low and dark, only letting through patches of sunlight, shifting and reforming in rays onto the ground.

"It's amazing," I whispered as the hostess led us to a table against the windows. Out in front of us, across grass, trees, roofs and boats, Old Town rose out of the water.

"I thought you'd like it," said Ludvig. "Not as many tourists make it out this far, so it's not too hard to get a table."

"Which way is my apartment?" I asked.

He pointed across the city in another direction. He leaned over the table, closer to me, pointing out other landmarks, too.

But all I could think about was the warmth of Niklas's large hands exploring my body the night before. At some point, I had awoken to a soft kiss on my shoulder. I had turned to move myself closer into his arms, only to find him fully aroused.

"*Please*," he had whispered in my ear. "I just want you so much."

He had entered me that way, wrapped in his arms, his body—

The waitress stared down at me, ending that thought. After we ordered, Ludvig turned to me with a look of brimming excitement.

"I have some news for you," he said. "I got you onto our team to cover the European football championships. I told the editor that you spoke Spanish, and he agreed you'd be a good addition. You're going to Spain with us. My boss will work out the ticket and the visa for you. We're leaving next week to get ourselves in place early."

I opened my mouth, but nothing came out.

"Isn't that great?" he said. He stared at me now with a kind of impatient expectation and then added, "It's a great opportunity for your career."

I blinked, trying to register what he had said.

"It's an amazing opportunity," I finally said. "It's just a bit of a surprise."

I saw a flash of irritation on his face, but a moment later it was gone.

"But we talked about it at Filip and Veronica's," he said quickly. "And I had to pull some strings to get you in. Since you don't have that much experience to your name."

He turned to look out the window, letting that last sentence linger between us. My face reddened, part embarrassment and part anger.

"And it pays well," he added. "Well enough to fund at least a few more vacation stops."

I wanted to tell him that my trip was a career move, not just a vacation, but it wasn't worth correcting him. I had, in fact, explained that when we met at Veronica's, but though he had heard the general idea of my plan, he clearly hadn't listened very hard.

"Thanks," I said. "I really do appreciate that you did this for me."

"So I can confirm with the editor that you're coming, right?" His eyes bore into me from across the table as he waited for my answer.

I swallowed.

"I'm not sure," I said. "I just need to think about it a little."

"Okay. Fine," he said, looking out the window. "Just let me know soon. I'll need to tell my boss and cancel your ticket right away if you're not coming."

I opened my mouth to apologize but then closed it again. The only thing I was sorry for was disappointing him, and this was a sentiment that irritated me the more I thought about it.

14
Complicated

For the second time in two days, I found myself pacing. This time, I was in my kitchen, waiting for the coffee to boil. On the table across from the stove, my laptop was open, waiting for me. After two weeks here in Sweden, I had turned in the first of my interviews, the one with Veronica. The response to the series was overwhelmingly positive. It was the break I needed for this career change to work.

Which meant I should be focusing on setting up the next interview.

Instead, my mind stubbornly returned to thoughts that had nothing to do with my career. Like the look on Niklas's face when he stormed out my door. Now, while I stood at the stove, waiting for the coffee to boil, my thoughts skipped back to the night we had spent together. My fingers tingled with the physical memory of his body as he stood over me, his mouth on mine, the ferocity lurking behind his slow kisses. His hands had explored my thighs and hips, pulling me closer.

But what had surprised me most was that fulfilling my desires with Niklas had left me wanting more. I had thought it would be the opposite. Over the years, I had had tastes of passing attractions. I had felt this kind of pull, the kind that could quickly evolve into infatuation: a hyper-awareness of a man's every move, each half-glance in my direction, each casual gesture. But it didn't take long to understand that initial attraction wasn't enough. I knew how easily the lure of infatuation faded when the fantasy of the unknown was gone. Nothing ever fit quite as well as I had imagined it.

This was different. Something about Niklas fit with me in a way I hadn't known was possible. I had assumed that acting on my fantasies would expose these encounters with Niklas for what they really were: lust, nothing more. But instead of casting the harsh light of reality, the long, beautiful night with Niklas stoked something deeper inside of me, something that I was trying hard to ignore, though I knew well that ignoring it was exactly what I should be doing.

More than once over the last two days, I had thought about how quickly professional athletes went through women, especially those with the kind of base, brutish sex appeal that Niklas had. It might as well be part of his job description. And I was leaving soon, so any glimmer of hope that he, too, felt something more than intense sexual attraction after our night together ultimately didn't matter. This couldn't be more than temporary.

I let out a deep sigh. My body might refuse to let the memory of Niklas's touch go, but I could coax my mind somewhere else. The empty email field at the top of the screen stared back at me. Veronica had sent me a few leads for my next interview, and all I had to do was send those people a message. But after the second article, I was on my own. Unless I took the Spain job.

True, Spain was an appealing stop as well, but I had the feeling that going there for the soccer championships would leave little room for my own work. Not for the kind of money Ludvig had alluded to. Even if I didn't have my own time, Ludvig would want to spend his time with me. I was almost sure that this was an unspoken part of the deal, a part that wouldn't go away easily. And then there was Niklas. Already, on this first stop in Stockholm, I was starting to hesitate about the trip I had wanted so badly. After the second interview, it would be time to move on from Sweden. And I wasn't ready for that. All because of a night with a man I hardly knew. A man who couldn't want the same things as I did...could he? No, I wasn't going to let myself fall into that same trap again.

The gray Stockholm sky filtered in through the balcony doors. Summer was here, but the weather gods seemed to have left the north. I had imagined that the midnight sun would bring continuous heat to this far corner of the globe, but I was wrong. Resting my chin on my hands, I closed my eyes and conjured up the magazine spread on Italy that I had held in my hands just a month ago, the gentle hills colored with the sage green of olive trees. I willed my mind back to the time when all I wanted to do was to explore the lush green of these valleys on foot, leaving a tiny *pensione* early in the morning with only a camera and enough food to last until dinner.

I let the image settle in my mind, feeling the hot Italian sun on my head and the soft dirt beneath my feet. Then I looked back at the computer screen and typed "Italian olive groves" in the search engine. The warmth of the photos flooded through me. Another college friend was living in the southern tip of Italy, the next stop if I followed my original interview itinerary.

This was what I wanted. It was still true. But what if my heart wanted more than one thing now?

*

I knocked for the second time on Veronica's door.

"Just a minute," called Veronica. "My hands are covered with paint."

I took a deep breath and let it out slowly. The irritation I had suppressed all day threatened to burst through, and my mind looped through my silent arguments with Ludvig: I didn't agree to travel to Spain back at Veronica and Filip's. In fact, if Ludvig had listened to me—and it was becoming increasingly obvious that he didn't—he would have heard that

Veronica, not I, was excited by the prospect of covering the soccer tournament.

The door opened, and in front of me, Veronica gave a warm smile. My shoulders relaxed at the sight of my friend.

"How was the U.S. game?"

"Fine," I said. "I just sent the photos off."

"'Fine'? You're going to have to muster up a little more enthusiasm if you want to pass as a sports photographer," said Veronica, wrinkling her nose. "Maybe 'gripping' or 'intense'?"

I raised a skeptical eyebrow at her. "I'm not sure those are the words the sporting world uses either."

"I'm from a country where most people have never even seen ice skates in person," she said, throwing up her hands. "What do you expect?"

Veronica closed the door and led the way down the long hall, into the warmth of her kitchen. "Coffee?"

"I think you've told me I'm under cultural obligation to accept."

Veronica gave a snort of laughter.

"I'm training you," she said. "It's the first step in my plan to get you to stay longer: indoctrinate you into Swedish habits."

Veronica put the coffee maker onto the stove and sat down across from me. I slumped in my chair, leaning my chin on my hand.

"Seriously," she said, drawing my other hand into hers and squeezing it. "Can you imagine yourself here for a little longer? I can work out an apartment for you. It wouldn't be difficult. Most people leave the city for rustic little cabins in the woods during the summer." Veronica wrinkled her nose and added, "Though I can't imagine why."

"Stay here in Sweden?" I asked quietly. "If I want to keep my dream job, the max I can stretch my stay in Sweden is a month, remember?"

I was trying not to allow the thought of more time with Niklas intrude on this conversation, but it was impossible. The question had nagged at me since the night with Niklas. I had told myself that kissing him would be enough to ease my growing infatuation with him. But a kiss wasn't enough. When I opened the door for Niklas, despite the anger on his face, something in me knew what would happen if I let him in. Pleasure. Sex. Intimacy. And I welcomed it. This feeling was something new, not driven by fear or a want for security. It was as if I were diving into the unknown.

Now after a night together, all I wanted was more of him. But even if he felt this way, too, what could I hope to come from this relationship? A couple more weeks of that aching mix of pleasure, want and withdrawal? After the month was over, I would find myself right back here. And letting go would be even harder.

"Maybe Ludvig can arrange something?" A smile teased at the corners of Veronica's mouth.

"He already has," I said with a frown. "That's what

I came over to talk about."

Veronica's eyes opened wider, and she leaned closer, cupping her hands around her coffee. "Well?"

"He's arranged for me to go to those soccer championships that he talked about in Spain with his team. He said they'll take care of everything, and the job pays well. It would be tight, but I'd probably be able to meet my magazine deadlines as well."

"So…" Veronica stared at me for a moment. "What's the problem? You don't sound excited at all."

"He didn't ask me if I wanted to go. Or if I could, for that matter," I said. Veronica continued to stare at me.

"He just organized it and then told me that I was supposed to go."

Veronica was still staring at me. "So you want to say no on principle? But you *can* go. And you want to, don't you?"

"I don't know," I said, looking out the window.

The clouds that had ominously loomed over the city all day were finally making good on their threat: The rain began. I watched the water hit the balcony doors, first in tiny, silent drops and then in larger splats. I looked back at Veronica.

"I know I *should* go. I need the money, and nothing legal is going to pay more than a job like this," I said with half a smile. "Plus, I feel like I owe it to Ludvig. Like he did me the favor of getting me the hockey passes, so in return, I should go along with his part of the plan, too. And he wants me to go to Spain with him."

"But?"

I shook my head slowly. "But I'm not a sports photographer, and I don't want to be one. I'm supposed to be devoting this time to my dream career, not getting sidetracked by another guy's plans for me. This trip was supposed to be about what I wanted to do."

I left Niklas out of this explanation. He shouldn't factor into my career plans.

Veronica raised her eyebrows. "But you need money. And you can do both. You just fly stand-by on the around-the-world ticket, so the timing doesn't matter."

I nodded impatiently.

"Right. But there's another problem," I said, slumping over table and resting my forehead in my hand. "I can feel that Ludvig's interest isn't just professional. He's never tried to kiss me or done anything overtly romantic, but the flowers, the nice restaurant, the favors... I can feel he wants something more. And to be honest, going to Spain with him would make me feel like some sort of...call girl."

Veronica's laugh caught me off guard, but it was loud and infectious, and soon I found myself laughing, too.

"*Dios mio*, Caroline, I really doubt that's what he has in mind. Well, maybe a little, but probably nothing serious," she finally said, still chuckling. "And why not give Ludvig a chance? Don't tell me you're holding out for the sexy hockey player across the hall."

I took a deep breath. "That's the other thing I wanted to tell you. Things between Niklas and me got a little more… complicated."

Just saying those words sent a sudden wave of memories through me—physical memories. His breath on my neck, hot and insistent. His fingers teasing my breast before he lifted it into his mouth. The hard muscles of his thighs pushing my legs open. I closed my eyes, willing the memories to stop there. But Veronica must have seen it on my face.

"Oooo, *Carolita*," she said, shaking her head. "Be careful. You know how those athletes are. They go through women like that." She snapped her fingers, drawing a little smile from me.

"I know, I know."

Part of me wanted to argue that Niklas was different, that things were different between us but in truth, the same thought had been running through my own mind over the past few days. This was exactly the kind of guy I had learned to stay away from back in college.

I looked at my friend carefully and said, "When we finished school, your father had everything set up for you. He had found a dealer for your paintings, and he had told your old boyfriend you were coming back. But you didn't go back. Instead, you left to travel through Europe with Filip, whom you hardly knew then, and ended up never going back to Mexico."

Veronica burst into laughter again. "*Sí*, I'm a terrible example."

I smiled. "But it all turned out well for you."

Veronica looked out her kitchen window and nodded. "But it all turned out well for me."

15
My price (in Euros)

You know how those athletes are.

Veronica's words looped through my head as I stared at the blank screen of my computer. Did I really want to know these details? Niklas had said that the worst things that were written about him weren't true— at least not in the way that they were written. What did that mean? Was he saying that he was wrongfully accused of something or that the media got the details wrong?

My heart pounded as I waited for the laptop screen to light up. Then, I typed the words into the search engine for the second time: *Niklas Almquist News*. And again, a band of photos appeared, on the ice and off. I scrolled down the page, past player statistics, until I found what I was looking for. Or, rather, what I hoped, irrationally, that I wouldn't find.

But there it was, listed in enough iterations on my screen that I couldn't ignore it. Ludvig hadn't exaggerated. I stared at the list of articles in front of me. The story was all over the Detroit news. With a deep breath, I clicked on one. Niklas's face was suddenly in front of me instead. The shot was taken outside at night, in front of a hospital I thought I recognized. And Niklas looked furious. The way I had seen him on the ice. The woman next to him had turned from the camera, but not enough to completely hide the swollen mess of her eye.

My mouth dropped open. *Shit.* Yes, this *was* really bad. I couldn't even bring myself to read the article. *Shit.*

The photo seemed to speak for itself, didn't it? I believed that photos captured parts of a person, right? If this photo truly captured a part of Niklas, I wanted nothing to do with him, no matter what kinds of feelings he stirred in me.

But was what I saw the truth? Or could I trust what he had told me, trust that there was something more to the story that would make me see this scene differently? Everything about my interactions with Niklas suggested he would protect me, not hurt me. Even that first day I had seen him in the park, before we met, he had made sure nothing happened with Baseball Cap. I had been over this reasoning so many times.

Still, his words came back to me: *Hockey brings out something in me, something I can't always control.* And he hadn't denied the incidents on the ice.

Should I give him a chance to explain? I lay my head on the kitchen table. I didn't know what to think.

*

Ludvig's car sped up the ramp onto the raised highway and then over the bridge past Old Town, towards the giant arena ahead of us. We were running late for the game, but I suspected this wasn't the only reason for Ludvig's sour mood. The sun had momentarily appeared from between the billowy clouds that spread across the city, shining down on the water and lighting up the buildings in front of me.

"I can't believe that I've been here this long and still haven't spent the day with my camera in Old Town," I said as we rode along the edge of the island. Walls of stone, brick and painted plaster rose up on either side of us, passing by too quickly for me to take them in.

"Old Town is mostly just little souvenir shops and overpriced restaurants, if you like that kind of thing," said Ludvig, not taking his eyes off the road. "But I guess it's worth a day just to say you've done it."

"Yep, souvenir shops and overpriced restaurants. That's what I'm looking for," I said with a wry smile.

I looked over at him, but he wasn't smiling, clearly not in the mood for humor. I drew in a breath but tried to keep my sigh silent, bracing myself for another tense car ride.

And then it hit me. I had been wrong about him: Ludvig wasn't nice. As soon as something—or someone—rattled that precious equilibrium enough, his placid exterior corroded in favor of carefully barbed comments and long, painful silences. I knew all of this only because I had years of intimate experience with it: Brad was the same, and, I realized, he wasn't actually nice, either. And I had accommodated him. I never would have put Brad and my relationship in these stark terms if Ludvig hadn't been sitting next to me now, with his clenched jaw and his white knuckles gripping the steering wheel. He was doing the exact same thing, and I could feel my own sinkingly familiar urge to placate him.

"I need to know if you're going to Spain by the end of the week. You have to tell me by then," he said suddenly.

I didn't answer.

Ludvig's little car shot out of a tunnel and crossed the last bridge, heading for the giant white ball in front of us. When we finally pulled into a parking space, Ludvig turned off the motor, but he didn't climb out. There a hint of uncertainty in his breath, as if he were just as uncomfortable as I was.

"I brought all the information for Spain if you're coming," he said, reaching into the back seat and returning with a small stack of papers. "The contract should be ready sometime later this week."

Though I had already made up my mind, I took the papers from him and looked down at them, though putting off the inevitable wasn't making me feel any better.

But what I saw in the middle of the page was a

number that made me gasp aloud. 30,000 Euros. I would be paid 30,000 Euros for a month of work. I wasn't sure about the exchange rate, but I knew enough to realize this was more than $30,000. More than I had made during the entire last year of work. Enough to do whatever I wanted for the rest of the trip. I would no longer have to cross off dream stops like Dubai, Japan and Hawaii from my list because of the costs. With my ticket already paid for, I could go anywhere.

I closed my eyes, suddenly unable to think through the situation clearly. I would never get an opportunity like this again. I couldn't turn it down.

Before my mind began to churn through all my doubts, before I had the time to change my mind, I opened my mouth and answered.

"Yes, I'll go."

It was done. I was going to Spain.

The tension I had felt from Ludvig suddenly transformed into enthusiasm. And before I understood what he was doing, he leaned over and kissed me on the cheek.

"Fantastic," he said, smiling. "You'll love it. We already have everything planned."

Ludvig was talking as both of us climbed out of the car, but I didn't take anything that he said in. All the debate and resolve of the last days had disappeared the moment I had seen the number 30,000. Now, my thoughts rushed back in, and they weren't forgiving.

Is 30,000 Euros my price? And if so, what is he

buying from me?

I swallowed the bitter taste in my mouth and tried to listen to Ludvig's words. But nothing he said made me feel any better.

*

On the walk from the parking lot to the arena, I couldn't stop thinking about it. I had said yes. What bothered me most was the position I now found myself in...the situation I had created for myself. At the bottom of Ludvig's offer was the question, *will you come to Spain with me?* I could feel it, and my gut answer to the more personal side of his question was, in no uncertain terms, *no*. But when faced with a large sum of money, I thought bitterly, the integrity of my answer crumbled. The fact that it was a business offer wasn't a consolation since I suspected he wouldn't have arranged this if he wasn't interested in the personal side, too.

The cloud of dark thoughts hovered as we walked over to the arena. But as soon as I entered, they dissipated. The smell of the ice hit me as we walked through the hallway, towards the rink, and I was swept up in the cheers and whistles of the crowd around me. As we walked into the arena, the lights went off, and a swirl of spotlights hit the ice. The announcer's voice echoed around in the darkness as Ludvig and I found places along the edge of the rink. Then, in a burst of music, the red-clad Swiss players poured out from the tunnel opposite from us and gathered on their side of the ice. The music stopped, and the announcer's voice returned. Music filled the arena again, and the yellow and blue Swedish jerseys appeared through the tunnel.

I steadied my breath and squinted, looking for Niklas across the ice. A messy swirl of desire and dread brewed inside of me. He had told me not to come, and here I was. With a huff of frustration, I tried to push away the nag of guilt at my blatant disregard for his request, to choose his private life or his public. Of course, he hadn't considered staying home—it was my career opportunity that should be given up.

Then I saw him. When he stepped onto the ice, the cheers of the crowd grew, and my heart pound harder. I had dragged myself to sporting events for four years of college, wondering why the people around me had *paid* to come, but this was different. I gripped my camera in anticipation.

The Swedish team circled my side of the ice, passing pucks back and forth and shooting at the goal. Niklas wove in and out between the other players with a puck gliding at the end of his stick. As he swerved around toward center ice, I lowered my camera, and his head turned away from the action for a moment. Over past the boards. Over to where I was standing. Niklas looked straight at me, though it happened so quickly that I wasn't completely sure he had registered me. But I had seen the look on his face before—this much I was certain of. His blue eyes were filled with intensity, the same hunger I had seen just before he had lifted me, carrying me into the bedroom. But this time, something else was there, something that made me turn away.

It didn't take long for the game to get underway. The rink was a mess of red players and yellow players racing by me, first in one direction and then in another. Despite all the hockey games I had been to in college, I had never bothered actually learning any of the rules beyond the most obvious ones. I paid attention to the referee's whistle only because it often indicated a moment of emotion, possibly one I could capture on camera.

But now, for the first time, I wanted to know how the game worked. As the clock counted down the minutes of the first period, I turned to Ludvig with my questions. Why was the Swiss team called offside? Why did the referee call a penalty for checking this time when only seconds before, another player got hit with an even harder blow, and the referee ignored it? Why would anyone not wear better face protection in a game like this? I no longer cared if these questions made me sound unprofessional; I just wanted to know.

Ludvig's face flushed as he took me through the game, pointing at each set of lines on the ice, lines I had mistaken as decorative. Ludvig's face grew increasingly animated as he went through different teams' strategies. As much as he looked down on the players in front of them, he clearly loved this game. I wanted to capture this, to study it.

"Do you mind if I take a couple photos of you

while you talk?" I interrupted him suddenly, mid-sentence.

He stopped and looked at me, confused.

"If you'd like, I suppose," he said in his proper British accent and then continued where he had left off.

The next period began, and the tempo on the rink pulsed through me as clumps of players skated by. I kept my eyes on Niklas as he pursued the hulking red figures, weaving his stick around the offensive players to steal the puck before shoving them into the boards. What surprised me most was just how fast he could skate. It was something I had missed in other games, but now, following Niklas around the rink, my mouth parted as the final seconds on the scoreboard ticked away. The first period ended, and the score was still tied, 0-0.

The players skated off the ice and into the narrow tunnels. When the last of them had disappeared, I turned back to Ludvig, who I found was staring at me with an expression that I couldn't quite read.

"You're watching him," said Ludvig, his expression guarded. "You're staring at him. First, he was in your apartment, and now you can't take your eyes off him."

Even if I had wanted to respond, I had no idea what to say.

Realizing that he wasn't getting a reply, Ludvig finally took his eyes off me and said, "Let's see what you got this period."

He took my camera out of my hand and slowly began scrolling through my photos. He squinted down at the tiny screen, looking for something—a photo that revealed some truth about Niklas and me? Apparently, it wasn't there. Finally, he gave my camera back. Then he turned on his own camera and found the photo he was looking for.

"You should have taken one of these," he said, handing it over.

It was Niklas, checking a Swiss player onto the boards.

"It happened right next to us," he said with another hint of accusation. "You had a good shot. And everyone else wants to see him like this, even if you don't."

I remained silent, looking at the photo, until Ludvig took his camera back from me.

"I'm getting something to eat," he said and walked away without bothering to wait for me.

*

The second period was rougher than the first. The players knocked each other against the boards over and over again skidding across the ice. Niklas's line filed off the rink and fell back onto the benches. They were getting tired, and the Swiss team didn't look any better. The score was still tied with no goals, and only a few shots had found their way to the goalies. Packs of players circled around in front of me, grunting, eyes flashing, fighting for the puck.

Niklas's line came back on the rink. They spread

out and shot forward against the Swiss line, passing the puck back and forth. Niklas stayed on the outside, passing it in and then taking it back over the line as the offensive players repositioned themselves, looking for a hole in the Swiss defense. The Swiss missed their opportunity to switch lines, and now they were wearing down, stuck on the defensive, fending off the shots and tips the Swedish team bombarded them with. Someone in yellow passed the puck back to Niklas, but this time, instead of looking for someone closer, he drew back his stick and swung, lifting the puck into the air, straight at the goal. A mess of yellow and red jerseys swarmed around the net, blocking the goalie's line of sight. By the time the goalie saw Niklas's shot, it was too late. The puck floated into the top corner of the net. Niklas had scored.

The spotlights flashed, and the sound of the crowd exploded in my ears. Niklas's teammates buried him in a giant swarm, and when they finally released him, I caught a glimpse of the open joy across his face I had seen before. Happiness. At that moment, he looked as if nothing else mattered to him.

The crowd was still on its feet when the puck dropped again. The Swiss passed back and forth but couldn't get the puck far enough down the ice. And the more they lost possession of the puck, the harder they seemed to check the Swedish players.

Down at the Swedish goal, Niklas curved his stick around to steal the puck, but before he could skate away, the Swiss player hooked his stick around Niklas's leg, bringing him to the ice. Ludvig had explained enough for me to understand that this was illegal, but the referee was momentarily distracted by two other players, yellow and red, shoving each other behind the goal. He didn't see the hook.

Niklas stood up, but instead of heading for the puck, which was already on his teammate's stick, he turned back to the Swiss player and skated toward him, much too fast. The Swiss player came at Niklas as well, and they crashed into each other. Niklas dropped his stick and grabbed a hold of the red jersey in front of him. The Swiss player pointed and yelled back. From somewhere beyond, the whistle blew, but before the referee could intervene, the Swiss player's glove was off. He drew back his fist and punched Niklas in the face.

Both teams swarmed around the two players, pulling them apart and yelling at each other. Niklas's back was to me, and he was bending over, holding his face. Blood dripped onto the ice, leaving a trail behind him as he slowly glided over to the long tunnel and off the rink.

"Nice," said Ludvig. "We're in a great position to get all this."

I turned my head away from the tunnel and looked back to Ludvig. He lowered his camera, revealing the glow of unabashed pleasure on his face.

16
What if I stayed?

I was dreading the ride home from the game. The last thing I needed right now was more time alone with Ludvig, but I was too exhausted to lug my camera and myself over to the subway station right now. Reluctantly, I climbed into his car and shut the door.

"That was the best game I've been to in a long time," said Ludvig, seemingly oblivious to my dampened mood.

I raised my eyebrow. "Aren't you supposed to be upset that Sweden lost?"

"Sure," he laughed. "A win would have been nice, too. But those fights are what everyone came for. And that's what makes the news. No one wants to look at photos of smiling hockey players making polite passes to each other. They want to see blood. And Almquist definitely gave it to us. You can count on that from him."

His mouth turned down at the corners as he spoke

Niklas's name aloud.

I had to admit that there was some truth in what Ludvig said. I, too, had felt the rush of the game as I watched Niklas weave around the rink and, yes, when he shoved the Swiss players against the boards and skated away with the puck. But the trail of blood that followed Niklas out of the arena was too much.

When I didn't respond, Ludvig turned, and finally he registered the grim look on my face. His expression tightened, and when he spoke again, his eyes bore into mine, as if to make sure I didn't miss his message.

"Those guys out there play the game and fight with each other because they love it. To be a hockey player, you have to care about the sport more than anything else, every single day of your life. All those guys out there on the rink? Nothing in their lives will ever come before hockey. And they have to practice that ruthlessness every day, on and off the ice. That's what makes them good."

Ludvig turned on the engine, but before he pulled out of the parking space, he turned to look at me one more time. "The players chose that life, just like you and I chose this one."

*

The car ride home was silent. I kept my head turned toward the window, wishing what Ludvig had said wasn't true. The car was small and stuffy, and I needed to get out. All I could think about was how to extricate myself from the mess I had gotten into. Ludvig stopped at the curb in front of my building, his face still hard and angry. He didn't say anything.

I let out a heavy sigh. My relationship with him was supposed to be professional. If he was angry at me because I was clearly more interested in Niklas, despite his very public faults, well, he'd just have to get in line. I was just as frustrated with myself about it.

"Thanks for the ride," I mumbled before I closed his car door.

I opened the heavy door of the apartment building and walked in. My steps echoed through the quiet stone hallway. After all I knew, after watching him today, how could I still be thinking about whether or not Niklas was home? Niklas, who was the subject in a photo far worse than I had imagined. But he had said it wasn't true. And nothing in the headlines suggested he was arrested, only that the circumstances looked bad. Really bad, as he had so bluntly told me. Should I give him a chance to explain? But what could he possibly say that could make me see that photo differently?

The night we had spent together, the way he had looked at me, held me, touched me, whispered my name, was so different, so far from this mess. When we were alone, it was as if none of these other things—hockey, Ludvig, my future, the photo—mattered. But that feeling didn't last. It couldn't. Even the next morning after he had spent the night, he had left early, the pull of hockey too great. And besides, I was leaving. How many times had I been through this debate in my mind?

I slowed at the bottom of the spiral stone staircase, Niklas's apartment only a flight away. The idea of knocking on his door felt both ill-conceived and ill-timed. Still, I wanted to see him. My footsteps clacked in the empty stairway. Then I came to my landing. Our landing. I took a deep breath.

I walked up to Niklas's door and listened. Nothing. I knocked. First, there was nothing, but then I heard what sounded like a door closing. Was it from his apartment? Did he hear my knock and retreat further away? I stood still, my resolve continuing to crumble. I knocked again, but this time I heard nothing but the pounding of my own heart.

The elevator jolted and clanked behind me. I listened to the motor until the tiny box appeared through the stained-glass window of the elevator doors. The gate opened, and Niklas stepped out.

He was freshly showered and wearing a button-up shirt and jeans. Across his left cheekbone was a long red cut, sealed shut with surgical tape. Niklas looked up at me, and what I saw in his eyes made my breath catch. His expression was open for only a moment, full of unguarded lust and anger and passion as he took in my unexpected presence. Then it all disappeared. He drew in his emotions, and in their place, he gave me the same steely look that I had seen when Ludvig appeared at my door, interrupting our last conversation.

"You're back late," he said, looking down at the

camera bag I had dropped at my feet. I looked at my watch. It was past dinnertime, which my empty stomach confirmed.

"How's your cheek?" I said, walking over to get a closer look.

"It hurts like hell, now that the anesthesia's wearing off."

"I saw it happen," I said quietly.

"I know," he answered. A glimmer of emotion broke through his hard blue eyes.

"Can we talk?" I said.

He didn't speak for a long time. Instead, he looked over towards the stairwell and out the windows until I was almost sure he wasn't going to answer. But then he nodded. His fingers brushed against my hand as he walked over to unlock his door, and his touch sent a familiar flutter through me. I hesitated. Yes, I wanted to go with him, though I had no idea what this decision meant. But I followed him in, and the door slammed shut.

Boxes lined the hallway and were scattered around the first room I could see, the living room, as if another moving truck had just arrived. The kitchen looked a little better. At least the boxes were opened, and a small stack of plates and glasses sat on the open shelves above the counter. Niklas took down a glass and poured himself a shot of whiskey.

"You want one?" he asked, looking across the room to where I was still standing.

I shook my head.

"Suit yourself," he said and drank down the amber liquid in one gulp.

He looked back up at me. "Your boyfriend's busy tonight? I guess I gave him something to write about."

His voice was low and rough, and a red flush was rising in his cheeks. His hand clenched the glass. He had an edge to him that I had seen a glimpse of when he came to my door the other day, confronting me with the photos I had taken of him. But this time, he didn't bother to hide his frustration.

"I'm not going to answer that," I said, my own cheeks getting hot, too. "I already told you that Ludvig is a colleague, nothing else to me."

Niklas's jaw unclenched a little. He took a deep breath and walked across the room until he was standing only inches away from me. I could feel the pull of the heat from his body. He still clutched the empty glass in his hand, his knuckles white around it, but his other hand reached for me, then stopped.

"Why did you come to the game?" he said. "I told you not to."

"And I should do what you tell me to do?" My eyes narrowed, daring him to answer yes.

"I wanted you to listen to me." He spoke with slow, icy deliberateness, his blue eyes dark and fixed on me. "I told you I can't mix hockey with something…something like this."

His head bent toward mine, and I found myself

staring at his full lips, my entire body wanting to taste them again. This was hardly the tone of our conversation, and, yet, I felt it as much as I felt anything else. I wanted to reach up and trace the cut across his cheekbone, the line of the scar above his eye.

I had decided to give Niklas a chance to explain. But, in truth, I came for more than that. I came because the giddy rush of being with him, even just once more, was too great to resist. And standing so close to him now, the pull between us was even stronger than before. Ludvig's words nagged at me again: *Nothing would ever come before hockey for him.* Being that person on the ice would always come first. That truth lay behind Niklas's success on the rink, and I couldn't lose sight of it.

Did he let me into his apartment out of some misplaced chivalric duty, because we had slept together? Had he changed his mind about wanting something more than a night? It was so easy to believe I could be just one in a long line of women that he spent the night with, only to move on after the next game. Or did he also feel this same physically consuming desire that made my whole self come alive? I stepped back, hoping that separating my body from his would help me think, but I felt the kitchen wall behind me, holding me in.

Finally, I drew in a breath and answered him.

"I barely even know you, and you're telling me what I should do?" The evenness in my voice surprised me.

I watched my words hit Niklas, and a mix of anger and hunger exploded on his face.

"No," he growled. "I'm telling you I can't handle this."

It took a moment for me to register what happened next. His arm jerked, and then there was a crash, something shattering against the far kitchen wall. He had thrown something across the room. The empty glass he had been holding, which now lay in shards on the kitchen floor. I looked from his glass to his hand and then back again at the floor, trying to process what he had done.

I couldn't move. What Ludvig had said about him, his aggression on the ice, the photo I had seen—these all came crashing together in my mind. My heart pounded through my whole body, and for the first time, I registered his towering figure with a twinge of fear.

He saw it, too. He closed his eyes and took a step back, his face suddenly pale. There was no other sound besides his breath, ragged and uneven.

"Oh, fuck," he whispered.

I swallowed. Should I leave, or did I still trust my most basic instinct—that he would protect me, not harm me? His face contorted with anguish.

"Is this how it is with you?" I asked softly. "I saw the photo."

He took another step backwards.

"And now you think I did that. That I'd do it to

you." He bent over and rested his hands on his knees, hanging his head down. "*Oh, fuck.*"

Niklas shook his head, and he slowly stood up. There was something else in his expression now. Fear?

"No, Caroline. No," he said, finally meeting my eyes. "This is exactly what I didn't want to happen."

I willed my voice steady. "When I saw the photo, it didn't seem to match the person I know, the person I let into my apartment and spent the night with. Until now," I said. "Should I be afraid of you?"

My words seemed to cause him physical pain, and his shoulders hunched, as if to contain it.

"*Please, no,*" he said, his voice heavy and low. "I didn't hurt that woman, and I would never, ever do anything to hurt you."

He winced as he spoke the words, and his hand raked through his hair. For a moment, he looked defeated. "Please, Caroline, can I come closer?"

I took a deep breath and nodded. He closed the distance between us, his eyes sad and pleading. He reached for my hand, and he held it softly in his.

"All along, this is what I've been scared of," he whispered. "That I'll turn into some sort of monster off the ice if I let these worlds get mixed up, if I let myself feel something...more. I've seen other guys step over the line, and I've tried so hard not to let it be me." He shook his head slowly. "I shouldn't have let you in tonight after a game. It was stupid and selfish."

"That scared me, Niklas. It wasn't okay." My voice

was barely there.

"No, Caroline, it wasn't okay." Niklas's voice was shaking now. "I know this could be the last time I ever touch you. You might walk out right now and never come back. And I wouldn't blame you."

He was putting the very worst of him, all his fears into words. I could see how much it hurt him, but he continued. "If I ever did make a move to hurt you, I would want you to never come back. I'm so afraid of what you think of me now. I get angry, aggressive on the rink. But I would never, ever hurt you or any other woman. And I promise I won't do anything that scares you again, either. Please give me one more chance. Just one."

He stroked my hair and pulled me in against his shaking body. One more chance. He had given me another chance when he suspected the worst of me...but this wasn't the same thing at all. He waited. I drew back to look at him again. In his eyes, I saw deep fear and regret, but I knew that wasn't a guarantee. Nothing was, in fact. Either I gave him another chance, or I left right now, forever.

I wasn't ready to leave. I wanted to understand this, to understand him. To remind both of us that the night we spent together was different. It was more. I wanted to kiss him, even if it was for the last time.

His lips were soft and infinitely tender, just barely touching mine, an apology waiting for my answer. I opened my mouth and kissed him back, still hungry for the taste of him. His fingers skimmed my sides in gentle, soothing strokes, and he trembled underneath the kiss. I brought my hands to his waist, and his muscles twitched at my touch. His kiss was more than an apology now; it was a promise, a promise of the things I had come for. A promise for more. My body answered his.

His mouth opened to mine, softly biting my lip between his teeth, no longer holding back his hunger. His lips grazed my neck, and a low rumble came from deep in his chest. Then, he froze, breaking off from the kiss. He took a step back, leaving us both panting. When he spoke, his voice was rough.

"I can't—" he began but then stopped. He drew in another harsh breath. "If you don't want to give me another chance, I understand. But you should go."

His eyes were hot when they met mine, and I could see it was taking all his strength to stay away from me. My eyes fell to his hands, balled into fists again. He was giving me a chance to back out. *You know what I am now*, he seemed to be saying. *Leave if you need to.*

But I didn't move. At that moment, I wanted him. All of him. And I trusted what was happening between us. Was that enough?

"One more chance," I finally said, looking straight into his eyes, and I swore to myself that it wouldn't be more than one. "I need to believe that I never have to fear you."

I closed the distance between us again. Lifting my

hand, and I ran my fingers over his hot skin. "I want this, Niklas," I whispered, my own voice shaky now.

His eyes were still fixed on me. He reached up and smoothed my hair. I closed my eyes as his lips found mine again, his tongue slowly exploring my mouth. Then his teeth scraped over my bottom lip, harder this time. He kissed my neck, drawing out flashes of hot lust that pulsed through me. His lips explored my shoulders, and his hands moved down my sides and onto my hips. My back hit the wall, this time with his hard, heavy body against mine. I pulled up his shirt and my fingers met his hot, bare skin. My fingers traced the tense muscles of his back.

He found the hem of my dress and moved his hand up the curve of my hip and the inside of my thigh. Slowly, he drew his fingers up until he reached the top.

Oh, God.

"Oh, Caroline, is that for me?" he growled in my ear, hints of sadness and uncertainty and pain still there. "Do you want me, right now?"

"Yes," I breathed.

I grasped at the buttons on his shirt, trying to steady my hands as I pulled them open. Heat radiated from the muscles across his chest, and his heart pounded as fast as mine.

Finally, I freed the last button. I ran my hands across his chest and over the expanse of his shoulders, opening his shirt. I pushed it down the taut muscles of his arms. I tugged the sleeves over his large hands, the knuckles red and raw. Slowly I traced lines back up his arms.

Niklas lifted his hand to my shoulders and pulled down the straps of my dress, letting it fall to the floor. Then he pushed away the straps of my bra. With his mouth he explored the places that the fabric of my dress had covered, first my shoulders, then down my chest. He found my nipple with his mouth and ran his tongue over it. Then his teeth. My legs were shaking, ready to give out, and I swayed back against the wall, waves of pleasure running through me. He reached around my back to undo the bra clasp, letting it fall to the floor, too.

He rested one arm on the wall, and his head hung above me, his forehead almost touching mine.

"My God, Caroline," he whispered, his voice, raw and low, sending a shiver through me. "You make me crazy. I can't stop thinking about the smell of your skin, your hair, your perfect breasts, the way you moan when I touch you."

His large hand smooth my hair. The heat from his fingers seared my shoulders. I reached for him, and his breath tightened as my hands slowly traveled down, over his stomach and to the buckle of his belt. I knelt down onto my dress and undid his buckle. Slowly, I unbuttoned and unzipped his jeans. Then I slid them down over his long, muscular legs, my palms flat against his hot skin. He stood completely still, every muscle of his body tense. I stripped off the rest of his clothes to reveal the last of him.

Shivers of anticipation ran through my body as I stared at this man in front of me. A hint of sadness still lingered in him, and I wanted to touch him everywhere, to close that distance, to connect with him in the most intimate way I could. I placed my hands on the thick muscles of his thighs and moved up slowly, over the dark blond hair that curled over them. As my hands moved further up, I came closer until I was only an inch away. I looked up at him. His mouth was parted, and his eyes were heavy with desire. Niklas suppressed most of a gasp, and his erection throbbed in front of me. Then with the touch of my lips, a low, torn groan escaped from his mouth. More groans, and then a strangled cry.

He lifted me roughly by the shoulders and kissed me hard, his body rigid against mine. Then he picked me up, but we only got as far as the living room doorway. He pressed me up against the door frame as his fingers slid inside my panties.

"Right now," he said, breathless, and I shuddered with pleasure.

Before I could finish nodding, he brought me down onto the soft, red carpet on the living room floor. His hands tight around my wrists, he held them over my head, and his mouth found my breasts again, sucking and nipping at them until I cried out. I moved under the weight of his grip, but his grasp was firm and strong, and he didn't let go. Instead, he opened my legs with his knee, and positioned himself. He stopped, waiting, his eyes dark, intense, searing into me. At that moment, our connection was stronger than anything I had felt before. Then, with a low groan, he pushed deep inside me. I gasped, full and already on the verge of ecstasy. He began with hard thrusts, watching my face with the same intensity I had seen on the ice, teetering on the edge of control. Sweat formed at his temples as he pushed harder and harder, the fiery determination of his eyes burning into me. And the harder he pushed, the more my body came alive underneath him.

He was stoking something inside me, something that grew hotter and hotter until it threatened to consume every part of me. I wrapped my legs around him, raising my hips to meet his. He pushed deeper inside of me, bringing me to the edge, watching me with a look of triumph on his face.

"That's right," he said, his voice low in my ear. He tilted my hips and found his way farther inside me, leading me over the edge.

I cried out, unrelenting waves of heat moving through me. My arms strained as I tried to break free, to somehow contain the ripples of pleasure washing over me. But he held me there. As I cried out from under him, the delicate balance of control Niklas had held burst, sending even more, uncontrollable waves of ecstasy through me. He surged and let out a torn growl, his hips giving their final thrusts. Then he fell to his elbows, his body shuddering over mine.

A ragged string of Swedish words came from his

mouth as I gasped in shaky breaths. I lay still, my body entwined with his, not willing to let go of the opening we had just found in each other. He let go of my wrists and smoothed the mess of wavy hair out of my face. Then he lowered himself onto the soft, red carpet next to me, keeping his body pressed against mine. I breathed in the heat from him. I turned my head towards his so our lips were almost touching.

He watched me warily.

"What is it?" I asked.

"I'm worried I was too rough," he whispered, "but you seemed to enjoy it as much as I did."

I smiled at him, and the worry lines on his forehead began to dissolve.

"Mmmm," I nodded slowly, smiling. "You can always ask."

"Was I too rough?"

I shook my head. "Nothing that I didn't thoroughly enjoy."

I brushed his hair out of his face. He no longer looked sad. In fact, on his face now was the beginnings of a look that bordered on smug satisfaction.

"What was it you just said to me in Swedish?"

Niklas raised his eyebrows and gave me a mischievous smile. "Someday I'll tell you. But not now."

We lay in silence, the breeze from the window cooling our bodies. I didn't want to move. I closed my eyes and let myself melt into his warm, solid body.

After a while, I shivered, this time from the cold. He propped himself up on his elbow.

"What I'd like now is a shower," he said, and his eyes drifted over the curves of my body. "And I'm hoping you'll join me. I want to see what you look like wet."

I felt him stir against me again, impossibly soon. I raised my eyebrows. "You just saw me wet." Then I buried my face in his chest and laughed. "I can't believe I just said that."

He chuckled, his broad chest moving as he held me into him, the tension from before gone. But neither of us had forgotten it. I was sure of that.

*

His room was empty aside from a tall wardrobe and his enormous bed. The long windows that lined one side of the room looked out onto the trees of Vasaparken. I hadn't been out to my early morning sanctuary in a while now. The string of hockey games seemed to have switched my body over to Swedish time, and I had slept through the last few nights. But not tonight.

I lay on my back with my eyes closed. Niklas's body covered my side, and his leg lay over mine, entwined. I was warm, despite the cold night air. His hand absently smoothed my hair over my shoulder.

"My whole body aches, and I can barely keep my eyes open, but I don't want to sleep," he whispered.

I opened my eyes. I reached up and touched the

surgical tape that cut across his cheek.

"The game," I said. "You played today. It feels so long ago. And then..." My voice trailed off, not knowing what to say about our volatile first minutes together that evening.

But I had said enough. Niklas's lips tightened. He brushed a wisp of hair behind my ear and then put his hand on my cheek.

"I'm so sorry," he said softly. "When I play hard, I—"

He stopped and shook his head. Then he took a deep breath.

"That's why I wanted you to stay away from me after the game. And I really tried to keep my distance. But there's something about you, the way you are with me, something I can't stay away from. When I opened the elevator gate earlier this evening, I told myself I wouldn't knock on your door. Not tonight, no matter how much I wanted to touch you, to be with you. But when I walked out of the elevator and saw you standing in front of me—"

"So your solution is for me to stay away when you get like this?" I asked, raising my eyebrows.

My voice was gentle, but the question was a challenge. This was his own logic, but when I spoke it, he seemed to hear the holes in it.

"No," he said, shaking his head. "You're right. It's not your job to stay away from me. It's my job to make sure I find a better way to take care of all these...feelings." He was quiet for a while. Finally, he gave me a wry smile. "I don't even know your last name."

I watched his beautiful blue eyes, finally open for me. Whatever this was that I had with Niklas, he was right: it was different. I felt the pull of him, his body, his voice, his hands, all tugging deep inside me, and I wanted to find my way closer to him, closer than the skin of our two bodies allowed. And he didn't even know my name.

"Mendoza," I whispered. "My last name is Mendoza."

I ran my hands through his dark blond hair and then gently pulled his mouth down to mine. His lips were warm and soft, but I could feel the emotion behind his kiss.

"You're making me crazy, Caroline Mendoza," he whispered as he lifted himself over me.

Clearly, he wasn't *that* tired.

*

"What comes next for the famous Niklas Almquist?" I asked with a hint of a smile.

Twilight, the endless dusk of the Swedish summer night, glowed through the window. Niklas shook his head and looked at the ceiling. He lay with his hands clasped behind his head, the long muscles of his arms flexed hard. I rested on my elbows next to him and watched his lips as he spoke. My hair spilled over onto his chest in a tangled mess.

"One year with Djurgården. Practice starts in September." His voice was quiet. "Sometime before that, I need to go back to Detroit and sell my house, ship back whatever I want to keep."

His eyes moved away from me, and the tone of his voice was flat.

"You don't want to do that?"

"I wasn't ready to leave the Red Wings. Though after the last year, I can't say I'm surprised. But hockey is my life. It's all I think about, all day, every day," he said. Then his expression softened and he looked back at me. "Well…it was all I used to think about."

His mouth curved into a smile.

"I can hardly believe you lived like a monk all those years." I tilted my head skeptically.

"Well, no," he chuckled, "but it's never interfered with hockey before. Even when I was together with women, I didn't think about them during the rest of my day." He glanced over at me. "I know that sounds pretty cold, but it wasn't something I did on purpose. It just happened. Everything I did was for the game. I just thought that's the way I was." He stopped and let his fingertips trace down my arm. "Now I'm not so sure."

His hand began to explore the curve of my breast, and my heart beat faster. But I stopped him, taking his hand in mine. I ran my fingers over the angry red of his knuckles, studying his long fingers, rough and scarred. His fourth finger looked as if it hadn't healed straight from a break. Then I linked my own fingers into his, letting them cover my hand. I raised his scarred fingers to my lips and kissed them.

"I'm afraid of how much I want you," I whispered. "I'm afraid of what this is."

*

"What am I going to do?" I said aloud.

The light of the full moon, shining through one of the long bedroom windows, had awoken me. It lit up Niklas's face as he drew in slow breaths, asleep. I fought the urge to touch him, to trace the shape of his face, to slide my hand over the muscles on his shoulders and down his long arms. Instead, I watched the steady thump of his pulse on his neck. I studied the curls at the ends of his sandy hair, his inexplicably dark eyelashes, the fullness of the lips that had explored my body. I studied each of the details, storing them in my memory for the day that was coming soon, the day I would leave.

I hadn't told Niklas about leaving, as if not speaking of my inevitable departure made it less real. I had worked too hard to pull myself away from Brad, and Niklas…well, he had a far more dangerous lure that seemed to be especially made for me. But even if I could find a way to continue my interviews while staying close, where would that get me? Would I hang around Stockholm a little longer until my infatuation with him died down? Because surely that's what this was—infatuation. True, it felt different, stronger than anything I had felt before, but after only two nights and a few chance encounters, what more could I call this?

A cold gust of wind blew through the balcony door, sending goose bumps across my bare arms. I untangled myself from the warmth of Niklas's embrace and climbed out of bed. Quietly, I closed the door, but I stayed by the window, looking out at the tall trees that swayed over Vasaparken. For just a moment, I allowed myself to complete the thought I had already pushed away once that night: What if my mystical world, the one with just Niklas and me, was real? What if I stayed here, right here with Niklas, forever?

I closed my eyes to enjoy the warmth of this idea, but even allowing this tiny wish into my world was too much. Immediately, a cascade of objections clamored in my mind, starting with this one: Look what happened the last time you put off what you wanted for a man. No, I couldn't do that to myself again. The urge to leave Niklas's apartment right then was strong, the urge to tear myself away from him before I no longer could.

I shivered, and my naked body begged me to move. Where were my clothes? In a pile on the kitchen floor. Not far from the broken glass. But that memory triggered a flash of something else, the memory of Niklas's lips on my shoulders as he slipped the straps of my dress off. I tried to push it away.

"What's going on, Caroline?" Niklas's voice was rough and filled with sleep.

"I was cold, so I closed the door," I said. A half-truth. Just a moment before, I had contemplated walking out of his apartment. Now, when I heard his voice, I couldn't bring myself to do it.

"Come back," he whispered.

He lifted the covers for me, revealing the rest of his body, and my body stirred. No, I definitely didn't want to leave now.

Slowly, I walked back over to his bed and crawled in, fitting myself into him once more. He wrapped his arm over me and pulled me closer, his heat spreading through my body. Soon, I could feel the steady rhythm of his breathing against me again, coaxing away the tension of the unknown future. But I lay awake for a long time after that, knowing that separating myself from Niklas was only going to get harder.

*

I awoke to the smell of bacon, the smell of my childhood weekend mornings. I opened my eyes, but it took a moment to orient myself in the stark whiteness of the room. Niklas's room. He had opened a window again to let in the cool morning air. It had to be his Nordic blood, made of an entirely different substance, more resistant to cold.

I sat up in bed and felt the tug of soreness all over my body. And with each tug came a flash of Niklas up against me. I closed my eyes and let the breeze blow over my skin.

I opened them again and looked around. My dress lay neatly on the corner of the bed. He must have put it there. I slipped it on and then walked down the hall to the kitchen. Niklas was standing in front of the stove, dressed in only jeans, attending to pans of bacon and eggs. All traces of glass on the floor were gone. My stomach rumbled, reminding me of just how long it had been since I had eaten.

Though my body was clearly telling me to walk across the room and kiss him, feeling the warmth of his skin, I stopped instead. I leaned against the doorway and watched him, letting that feeling of warmth, of tenderness sit with me, drawing it out. This was the man I wanted, no one else. Why did Niklas speak to something deep inside me?

There was a lightness to the way he moved, a contentment that I hadn't seen in him yet. He turned around to grab bread from the other counter and caught sight of me. His smile was open and warm.

"An American breakfast, just for you. I'd come over and kiss you, but there's a lot going on right now," he said, gesturing to the food.

His eyes wandered from my face down to my breasts, where my bra was conspicuously missing. He raised his eyebrows and then turned back to put the bread in the toaster.

"Or maybe I'd do a little more than kiss you," he said. I could hear he was smiling.

I sat down at the kitchen table. Niklas grabbed two plates and began to serve the food. He placed one plate in front of me and then leaned down for a soft, warm kiss. Just as my hunger began to take a back seat to other wants, he broke away and walked back over to the counter.

"I don't know how you like your coffee," he said. "Milk? Sugar?"

"Just milk," I said as he sat down opposite from me. "Thank you."

"I figured you'd be hungry," he said and then added, "and tired."

I thought I saw another smug look of satisfaction cross his face before he looked down to take his first bite.

"And you?"

Niklas laughed. "I'm exhausted. In every possible way. But I have a few things to do today." He took a bite of his toast. "Listen, I want to do things right with you. I don't want to just meet in the hall and then spend the night together." His lips curved up into a smile and he added, "Not that I'm complaining."

I raised my eyebrows and laughed.

"This isn't coming out right." He chuckled. "What I'm trying to do is ask you to have dinner with me tonight."

"Are you asking me out on a date?"

"Out?" The smile faded a little from Niklas's face. Mine must have too because he quickly added, "Yes, we can go out. We'll give it a try."

"What's the problem?" I asked.

He shook his head. "Going out isn't always very private for me."

"And the famous Niklas Almquist doesn't like to mix public and private," I said, "so he'd rather stay holed up in his apartment when he's off the ice?"

Niklas gave my knee a quick squeeze under the table, right in the most ticklish spot, eliciting a yelp.

"That's right," he said with a wicked smile. "And I'm looking for someone to lock up in here with me."

He grabbed his plate, which he had mysteriously cleaned in a matter of minutes, and stood up. But before heading back to the stove, he bent down and gave me another kiss, even longer and deeper than the last. My fork clattered onto the plate as I reached up to move my hands over his bare chest. His skin was hot and alive under my touch.

He broke off the kiss and gave me a look that was definitely smug. "Have I convinced you to come to dinner?"

I nodded, still catching my breath.

Niklas loaded up his plate again and sat down, eating with the same eager intensity as he had before. "Actually," he said between bites, "I know a little restaurant on Södermalm with great homemade pasta. I can call and get us a table. That is, if you like Italian."

He stopped eating and looked at me.

"Are you sure you're up for going out?" I asked.

He raised an eyebrow. "Do I get to take you home after?"

Now it was my turn to squeeze his knee, though my hand barely spanned its width, and his thick muscles didn't seem to move under my effort.

"You can do a lot better than that," he said with a straight face, "just try higher up."

17
Dios Mio

The apartment was quiet. The rain clouds had passed over the city, leaving behind still, heavy air that lurked outside my balcony door. I sat at the kitchen table, waiting for Veronica's knock. My laptop was open, and the beginning of my second article waited for me on the screen. I was trying hard to concentrate on something besides Niklas...and failing.

I stood up and cleaned the stovetop coffee pot. If I had learned anything about Stockholm in the last few weeks, it was that guests were served coffee when they came over. Even Mexican transplant guests. I had just refilled the compartments and screwed the contraption back together when Veronica's knock finally echoed down the front hall.

"Are you now so busy that I have to plan ahead to see you, *Carolita*?" Veronica asked, kissing me on the cheek.

"I'm never too busy to see you," I said, leading my friend down the hall and into the kitchen. "I just wasn't near my phone last night."

"Well, I know I wasn't the only one you were ignoring," said Veronica. "Ludvig called to see if I knew where you were. He said it was important, that he had left two messages."

"What did you say?"

"That my friend was a fool to blow off any guy offering her a job that pays her the kind of money she desperately needs," she said.

My face flushed. "What—"

But Veronica burst into laughter. "*Dios mio*, calm down. Do you really think I'd say that? I told him I didn't know."

I started laughing, too.

"But I think I do know where you were." Veronica shook her head. "Caroline, what are you doing to yourself? You're leaving soon."

I closed my eyes and let out a sigh.

"You did tell Niklas that you're leaving, didn't you?" Veronica stared at me. "Tell me you told him."

I shook my head slowly.

"Why not?"

The coffee pot gurgled. I took it off the stove and filled up two cups. I brought them over to the table and sat down across from my friend. Then I took a deep breath. "I guess I just don't want this to end. And I'm scared I'm going to do something stupid like forget my plans, the ones that I've waited for for years, and throw myself at a man I only met a few weeks ago."

Veronica raised her eyebrows and added, "A very sexy man."

I let out a laugh.

"Yes, a very, very sexy man. But he's more than sexy," I said. "There's something about the way he is that just feels right. I don't know how else to say it."

"Oh, no, *Carolita.*"

"I know, I know," I said, waving my friend off. My smile faded. "Here's the worst thing: right now, there's a part of me that's ready to give up everything else just to stay with Niklas a little longer, just to find out if this is something real. The magazine job, the career possibilities, everything. And the more I'm with him, the more I feel it. But I swore to myself that I'd never do that again. I'm not giving up a part of myself."

Veronica gave me a rare look of seriousness. "It shouldn't feel like that."

"You're right," I said. Then I rolled my eyes. "Is this what you came over to tell me?"

"Oh," gasped Veronica, "I almost forgot. And it's bad news. I got a call from the owners of this apartment: Tommy broke his foot when they were hiking. It happened a few days ago, and now that the swelling has gone down, he wants to come home."

"How soon?" I asked.

"Sunday."

I blinked at her, registering what this meant.

Sunday. Three days from now. And two nights. I had two nights left to stay in the apartment across from Niklas's. Two nights left of my life here, two nights to figure out what I wanted to do.

Veronica was still staring at me.

"You know you can stay with us before you go to Spain, don't you?" she said quietly. "I don't want you to leave, either."

I opened my mouth to answer, but my phone rang before I could speak. I flipped it over and read the name across the screen: Ludvig. I stared at the phone and then looked back at Veronica, who gave me an impatient glare.

Finally, I pushed the talk button.

"Caroline, you didn't answer your phone yesterday."

"I know."

He waited for me to explain, but I didn't say anything. After a couple moments of silence, he continued. "Listen, my boss wants us to get together for dinner tonight, the whole European Cup coverage team. He's bringing the contracts and itineraries, and he has some specific assignments."

The line was quiet again. He was still waiting for me to confirm.

"I can't make it," I said softly.

"What?"

I knew by the sharpness in his voice that he had heard me, but I repeated it anyway. "This is really short notice. I can't make it tonight. There's something else I have to do."

"Something more important?"

I swallowed. "Yes, it's important."

Ludvig was silent for a long time. Then he said, "I'll call you later," and hung up.

I put down the phone and looked up at Veronica. Though my friend had only heard my half of the conversation, the look on her face suggested it was enough. Veronica shook her head.

"If you were looking for a little more excitement when you left Brad, you certainly got it."

I suddenly felt exhausted.

"I'm getting exactly the kinds of opportunities I came here for," I said. "So why am I debating the same career vs. guy thing?"

She smiled a little. "Maybe it doesn't have to be either/or."

"I wish."

But I just couldn't see how I could have both. In my heart, I wanted two different things, one that took me away from Stockholm and one that kept me here. And my logical mind already knew which one I should choose.

18
Tonight, I'm yours

I stepped out of the taxi and onto the wet sidewalk. Rain had fallen in bursts all afternoon, but the evening sky was bright and clear. I reached through the front window to hand the driver a wad of money, but Niklas covered my hand with his.

"Please, I want to take you out tonight," he said softly and handed the driver the fare. Then he smoothed my hair and let his lips brush against mine. The connection between us was growing stronger. It had felt odd to step out of the building with him, as if I wasn't quite sure the Niklas I knew would still be the same man off our apartment floor. But here he was, and his body next to mine was a constant reminder.

"The place is across the street, right there," he said, pointing.

Niklas grabbed my hand, and we ran across four lanes of traffic, towards the warm glow of a tiny restaurant. He held the door open, and I stepped in. I took a deep breath, trying to relax. Still, there was something that felt different about Niklas now that we were out, something guarded. I wasn't sure I could get used to it.

"I'm going to the rest room," I said, pointing at the doors in the hallway next to us. "I'll come find the table."

I closed the door behind me and let out a deep breath. Why was I so nervous, more nervous than I had been when he stepped out of the elevator the night before? I looked at myself in the bathroom mirror. It was hard to believe that only the night before I had walked into his apartment, wondering if I would find what I had hoped for. Something had shifted during the night, something that took us beyond just a hot hook-up, into other, murkier territory.

I had felt that same pull less than an hour ago when I opened my apartment door. Niklas had leaned against the door frame, freshly showered and in jeans and a button-down blue shirt that matched his eyes. He looked polished, like he did on the day of the press conference, but he was smiling—a real smile—and his eyes were fixed on me. His slow, deep kiss seemed to say *tonight I'm yours*, and that promise echoed through my body. For a moment, I regretted my suggestion that we go out.

It was the remains of this kiss, lingering on my lips, that had slowly transformed into a knot in the pit of my stomach: Tonight, I was about to disturb this delicate connection between us, so new and raw. It wasn't just his guarded look that had made me nervous. I couldn't put it off anymore. I needed to tell him about Spain. I had already waited too long.

I ran my hand through my hair in an attempt to tame the curls that had sprung up, taking on a life of their own in the humid night air. Then, with another deep breath, I opened the door and entered the restaurant.

The room was long and dark with private little nooks along the edges. Niklas's kind of place, with the air of privacy. The hostess wasn't at her station, so I let my eyes adjust and scanned the room. Then I saw him. Them. Niklas was seated in one of the last alcoves along the wall, and a woman was bending over in front of him, writing something and giving him a deliberate view down the front of her shirt at her large breasts. Her long, blond hair fell over her shoulders, and her miniskirt covered little of her tanned legs. Pretty much the opposite of me. She put down the pen and stood up. Then, with a smile, she walked over to a table across the room to join her friend. After taking her seat, the woman turned back to Niklas for a sexy smile.

My nails dug into my hands as I watched the scene play out in front of me. The woman was clearly making herself available to Niklas. Niklas looked down at the table and back up again, finding my eyes.

My gut told me to walk out of the restaurant, to get away from this sinking feeling. I had left this kind of guy behind in college. The kind of guy that had driven me to Brad in the first place. Why had I thought that Niklas would be different? I stood, frozen in place, as Niklas crossed the restaurant. He took my hand and led me to the table in a way that suggested he wouldn't take no for an answer. But instead of sitting down, I stopped in front of our alcove and looked down at the tiny scrap of paper that Niklas didn't bother to hide. On it was a phone number, the name *Marie* and three words in Swedish, the middle word double underlined.

"What does it say?" I said, my voice even.

He gave me a long, hard look. "Do you really want to know?"

No, I didn't.

"I do."

"It says, *Marie, your biggest fan.*"

At another time, the blatant crassness of the message might have seemed funny, but nothing about it seemed funny at this moment. Silence hung in the air.

"Please, Caroline, sit down. Please don't leave. *Please.*"

That was, in fact, what I was about to do: leave. But I heard something in his last *please*, something that made it hard to walk out on him. I frowned and sat down. The waitress brought a bottle of wine to the table that Niklas apparently had ordered before I came. She opened her mouth to speak, but after a look at our faces, she disappeared again.

"I'm sorry," he said. He kept his voice calm, but I

could hear impatience and frustration lurking behind it. "It happens. Not a lot, but it happens."

"And I don't suppose you said, 'I'm here with someone,' or else she wouldn't have left her number." My voice was rising, but I didn't care.

Niklas closed his eyes and shook his head. "You're right, I didn't."

"So you took her number, like a back-up plan for tonight?"

His face darkened, and his eyes blazed at me in anger.

"What are you saying?" he growled. "You think I would do that to you? I didn't tell her about you out of respect for *you*. Then you would be right there in the spotlight, too."

Oh. I let out a deep breath, trying to think rationally. I *did* believe him. I didn't really think that he would encourage another woman's attention in the middle of our evening together. It wasn't even that I was jealous, not really. But something inside revolted at the thought of being a part of this kind of competition for his attention.

Niklas was no longer trying to hide his frustration. "Listen, I thought this part of playing hockey would be better back here in Sweden, but it's not; it's just different. My public life is a mess, and I don't want you to get tangled up in it unless you're sure you want to be. These kinds of things get twisted and then—"

He broke off his sentence and ran his hand through

his hair. Heat rose on my face as his explanation sank in.

"Look, Caroline, I can understand if you don't want anything to do with this," he said. His expression had softened, and he reached across the small table for my hand, which was still balled up next to my plate. "I love hockey, but playing means my life isn't always my own. That's the trade-off." He paused and then added, "This is why I didn't want to go out tonight."

I swallowed hard and said, "So you just stay away from anything public? No dates, no nothing."

Maybe I should have offered understanding, but I was still reeling from watching that scene from across the restaurant. The woman was a stereotype of a man's fantasy hook-up, and seeing Niklas respond, even with good intentions…it still hurt. Even after just two nights together.

Niklas's voice was full of emotion when he spoke again. "I don't know where this is going or even what this is between us. I don't even know how long you're staying in Stockholm. I'm trying to figure it all out. I just don't want to hurt you."

He let out a deep breath, and when he continued, his voice softer. "My idea was that we could spend some time together, time alone, before we have to face this." He gestured to the scrap of paper that still lay, face up, on the table. "I'm finishing up a few things this week, but then I'll be free. Maybe we can rent a boat and drive out onto the archipelago, find a cabin somewhere and spend time together, just the two of us. Everything just feels so…so right when it's just us. We can come into the city for the games you need to cover and then go back out."

Oh, God, I wanted that with him. So badly.

For the first time since we had stepped into the restaurant, Niklas's face relaxed, and he met my eyes with a smile that should have filled me with happiness. Instead, it sank, heavy inside me.

"Niklas," I said quietly, unable to meet his eyes any longer. "I have something to tell you, something I should have told you before now."

The smile slowly left his face.

"I—I took a job covering a soccer tournament in Spain. It starts in a few days."

He was silent, and his gaze weighed on me, but I kept my eyes on my plate.

"And today Veronica told me that Tommy and Annika need their apartment back on Sunday."

More silence. I took a deep breath and looked up at Niklas. He opened his mouth, started to say something, but then closed it again. He remained silent, and when I glanced up at him, he was looking at me with eyes sad and dark.

"I had to leave sometime," I whispered. "But I really don't want to leave you."

It hurt just to say these words. The waitress, who had been hovering in the corner, seized the apparent break in conversation to approach us. She said something in Swedish, and Niklas answered.

"Are you ready to order?" he asked.

I hadn't even looked at the menu, and food was the last thing on my mind. I glanced down at the paper in front of me and skimmed the foreign text: Italian and Swedish, I guessed, and even my Spanish wasn't helping much.

"Is this pasta with seafood?" I whispered to Niklas, pointing at the menu. "That's what I want."

Niklas nodded and spoke to the waitress in Swedish, and she disappeared back into the kitchen.

Now it was just the two of us. Silent. I searched for something to say to make the situation better, but I came up with nothing. What was going on inside his mind? I knew there was little chance he'd get angry at me in a public place like this, and yet I almost wanted him to. At least I would know what he was thinking. Finally, I couldn't stand it any longer.

"I should have told you earlier," I said. Then the words came tumbling out. "I got the offer a few days ago, and I wasn't sure I wanted to go, but I really need the money to travel. Yesterday, I still wasn't sure, but Ludvig said he needed an answer, so I said yes."

"Ludvig with the flowers?" Niklas was watching me carefully now.

I nodded slowly.

"And you're going to Spain with him?"

I searched Niklas's voice for anger, but instead it was hard and detached.

"Yes, but it has nothing to do with him," I said quietly. "His boss made me an offer I couldn't afford to turn down."

I waited for Niklas to say something else, but he didn't. Now there was only surprise and hurt on his face, neither of which he made any effort to hide. The pit in my stomach was growing, and I didn't know what to do about it.

"I'm really, really sorry, Niklas," I said softly. "We barely know each other, but the truth is that I don't want to leave you. I didn't tell you because all of these things came so fast, and I didn't want it to be like this. And I also know how long it took me to start this trip. It's something I've wanted to do since I was in college, but it's taken years for me to leave my life in Michigan and venture out on my own. How can I give it up so easily?" I looked at him, silently begging him to understand. "I keep waiting for something to happen so that I don't have to decide between the things I want."

"But you already decided," he said.

He still sounded detached, almost as if he were just talking to himself. I opened my mouth to disagree but closed it again. I viewed the job in Spain as a spontaneous opportunity that I had jumped on, not a choice that I had carefully weighed among the other possibilities. I had told myself that the job was just temporary, that all the other things I wanted might still be waiting for me when I returned.

And yet Niklas was right. I made a decision. And

with that decision came the risk that none of the other paths would be open if I returned. The job might lead to another, one that dangled even more possibilities in front of me, one that would make it even harder to break from the path I had started down.

"You're right," I said. "I said yes to this job. But that doesn't make it a good decision. In fact, it feels like a really bad one right now."

He looked at me for a while, and then I saw something change in his face. Some of the coldness and hurt melted, and in its place, his eyes had a glint of what I had seen on the ice and then later, much closer up, though I didn't know what to call it—resolve? But the look disappeared before I could figure it out. I was left with the sense that he had made up his mind about something.

He reached across the table for my hand and held in his as he teased my fingers into his large, warm palm. When he spoke, his voice was low and tender.

"Okay, we'll do this your way," he said. "We'll wait and see what happens."

We sat that way until the waitress reappeared, this time with our meal, and the sight of food made my mouth water. I was suddenly starving. Niklas let go of my hand, and the waitress set the steaming plates of pasta in front of us, triggering a loud growl from my stomach.

He chuckled and wrapped his legs gently around mine. I picked up my fork and let the warmth of our tentative truce fill me as I started to eat. We didn't say anything, but it wasn't words that connected us. That feeling from back in his apartment returned, the feeling that we were building our own world together, and it made something as simple as eating dinner into more. By the time I looked up again, Niklas was finishing off the last of the formerly heaping bowl of pasta in front of him. He looked from his plate to mine and then back up at me with a hint of red in his cheeks.

"Sorry. When it's hockey season, I'm hungry all the time," he said, glancing down at his now-empty plate. "If I'm going out, I usually have a meal before I leave just so that I can eat like a regular person. But tonight, I was too... I didn't feel like eating. And this is what I get."

He was finally smiling at me again, and I laughed with relief. We were finding our way back to each other.

"If you don't mind, I think I need another course," he said, searching for the waitress.

I looked down at my meal, most of which was still there, and nodded.

The waitress approached and then, after a few more exchanges in Swedish, she left.

"I can't believe how well you speak English," I said.

"We start learning it in first grade here in Sweden," he said, "but most of what I know came from living in Detroit."

I shook my head. "My Spanish is terrible, and I've been listening to it for my whole life. Something about it just doesn't click for me. I can't imagine learning a language I didn't grow up with."

Niklas raised an eyebrow and said in a low, teasing voice, "Maybe you just need the right teacher."

"Is that so?" I could think of plenty of things in addition to language I'd love to learn with him, but none of them made for appropriate dinner conversation.

"Was it hard to leave Sweden and move to the US?" I asked.

Niklas leaned back in his chair. "In a way I guess it was. Everything looked different, bigger—the roads, the yards, the supermarkets, even the cereal boxes. A little like I was Alice in Wonderland. And people in the U.S. are a lot more outgoing than in Sweden. People expected me to talk all the time—neighbors, people waiting in line at the post office, everywhere. At first I went out of my way to avoid them, but it didn't work," he said, chuckling. "I must have been the worst neighbor that area had ever seen. And I had to speak English all the time. My brain felt like it was going to explode. After being out for a few hours, I'd lock myself in my house to try to regain my sanity.

"So, yes, the move was hard. But I didn't think about it that way at the time. All I ever wanted was to play in the NHL since I was old enough to watch it on TV. All the difficulties of moving to another country were just minor inconveniences when I thought about the kind of hockey I got to play."

"What did your parents think?" I asked. He had never spoken of his family, I realized. And the one time I had asked, he had put me off.

Niklas was silent for a moment before he said, "My parents divorced when I was 10. My father moved away with his new wife, and that was that—until I started playing in the top league here in Sweden. As you might imagine, he was thrilled. Suddenly, he was interested in having a son again." I stopped eating and looked at him carefully. His wry smile belied the sadness in his voice.

"My mother was more ambivalent. On the one hand, she was just as invested in my hockey career as I was. I went through some rough years, got into some trouble for a while until hockey took over. I can't imagine what I'd have gotten into if I hadn't had somewhere to take out all my frustrations. The same thought probably crossed her mind, too. But she wasn't sure that the NHL was the right place for me. She didn't think I'd ever come back. Lucky for her, things didn't turn out that way."

The same sadness was still in his voice.

"And now you're back playing for your old Swedish team?"

"For a year, maybe more, while I figure out what I'm going to do after that. Something that keeps me out of trouble." He laughed a little. "I can't imagine my life without hockey. It's hard knowing that I'm 30 years old, and my best years are already behind me."

The waitress approached the table with another dish, this one with chicken, polenta and some sort of tomato sauce. She set it down in front of Niklas.

"I was made for Italian eating, the long meals with lots of courses," he said smiling. After a few hungry bites, he asked, "And what about you? Why a trip around the world?"

"Adventure?" I smiled at him. "Freedom. A change from Michigan."

Niklas smiled. "True, but plenty of trips would be a change from Michigan. Where will you go after you finish the magazine job? With your ticket, you don't even have to decide where you're going yet, right?"

He really wanted to know about me. His eyes were fixed on mine, gentle, waiting, as if he were trying to unravel the mystery of me, just as I had been trying to do with him.

"The truth is that I don't know what will happen after this summer. I guess it's not so different from what you were just talking about," I said slowly. "My life back in Michigan felt over, just a long stretch of hazy sameness in front of me. All compromises, nothing I truly wanted. Though now I seem to have the opposite problem: too many things I want."

I hadn't actually put all of this into words before, and I wasn't sure I even understood all the wants and fears that had driven me here.

"My father has a good life. He has a good job and a nice house, and he and my mother love each other so much. I can see they still do, even after almost thirty years together. But there's a part of him that is still in Mexico, a part of him that he's missing.

"One night when I was in high school, I came home to find him dozing off on the couch with a beer can in one hand, listening to ranchero music. He never did that kind of thing. He waited up for me, but not drinking. So I sat down next to him, and he woke up looking startled, as if he wasn't quite sure where he was."

I glanced up to see if Niklas's eyes were glazing over with boredom, but instead I found him gazing even more intently at me. I took a deep breath and continued.

""'Are you sorry you left Mexico?' I asked. He shook his head and gestured with his hands, forgetting about the beer can. It spilled on the couch, but for once he didn't seem to care.

"'No, no, *mi amor*,' he said. He always called me that, *my love*. 'I couldn't stay when there was so much more out there in the world. I felt like that ever since I was little. My brothers weren't the same, and for a long time I thought there was something wrong with me. No, I couldn't stay in Mexico. But it's still my home, and my family still lives there. That part will never get easier.'"

I gave Niklas a half smile.

"I guess I got that same gene from my father," I said, "I wanted to be a part of the rest of the world, but I didn't want to leave and have that same sadness follow me, just like it followed him. When I saw the magazine job, I applied for it, knowing I was sacrificing my relationship with Brad and leaving my friends and family, but I did it anyway. It seemed like the perfect solution. I could take a year off, see the world, and come back to where I started, never having to say goodbye forever like my father did. All the adventure, none of the risk. Though—"

I stopped, hesitant to finish.

"Though what?" he asked softly.

I swallowed. "Though the 'no risk' part isn't working out the way I thought it would."

His eyes flickered again with a hint of hope. He nodded at me and then took the last bite of his second course. I leaned back in my chair and took a drink of my wine. Niklas's legs were still wrapped around mine, reminding me of the nearness of his body.

A man in a well-cut pinstriped suit approached the table, his eyes fixed on Niklas. He cleared our plates and nodded at me. Then he began talking to Niklas in Swedish. The conversation was lost on me, but I watched Niklas's face change as the conversation progressed. His mouth tightened as he silently took in whatever the man was saying to him. But that look didn't last. He took a breath and unclenched his teeth, and I instead saw the person I had seen at the press conference emerge: Niklas in front of a crowd. He took control of the conversation, asking the man something and nodding in response. Then, after a few quick exchanges, the man left.

As soon as the guy's back was turned, Niklas's mouth tightened into a frown. His legs had pulled away from mine, and he was sitting rigid in his chair. I stared at him, waiting for some clarification, but he said nothing.

"What happened?" I finally asked.

Niklas looked up at me in surprise, as if he had momentarily forgotten the conversation had taken place in Swedish, that I didn't understand a word of it.

"He's the owner. He was telling me about an article in *Expressen*, a newspaper. He's going to get it."

The man in the pinstriped suit returned with a newspaper. He laid it down in front of Niklas, and then, with an apologetic look, he retreated back to the kitchen.

I looked down at the paper in front of Niklas, folded open to the section labeled "Sport." I couldn't read a word of the title or the article itself, but the photo was clear enough: Niklas, full of rage, struggling to break out of the restraining arms of his teammates. But something more caught my attention. A name, in bold, right at the top of the article: Ludvig Sundin. *Ludvig.*

One look at Niklas's clenched jaw told me all I needed to know. The article wasn't about anything good. After a few minutes, he turned over the newspaper. He unclenched his fists and ran his hand through his hair. Finally, he looked back up at me, slowly shaking his head.

"I was hoping I had left all this behind in Detroit," he said, gesturing at the newspaper in disgust, "but it seems to have followed me here."

Two questions came to me at that moment. I understood that this wasn't the time for the first one, the question I had been harboring since the day he had knocked on my apartment door and interrupted my internet search: What happened back in Detroit?

So I asked my second question.

"What does the article say?"

"I'll read you the title," said Niklas with a joyless smile. "'Almquist: Asset or Liability?' You can guess which side this writer falls on."

I already knew. I had known what Ludvig thought of hockey players in general and Niklas in particular since the first day I had stood with him beside the ice. In fact, I had been standing next to Ludvig when he took the photo that stared up at us from the newspaper right now. The thought grated on me, opening another uncomfortable question: Was I somehow involved in Ludvig's particular interest in Niklas's vulnerabilities? I couldn't forget the look on Ludvig's face when he had come over to pick me up and found Niklas there. Jealousy. That's what I had seen. I was sure of it now.

When I looked up again, Niklas was watching me. When he finally spoke, his voice was rough and sad. "Would you mind if we went somewhere else for dessert? I want to walk a while."

I raised my eyebrows. "Dessert?"

Niklas managed a little smile. "Am I the only one who's still hungry?"

*

Though the sun had not yet hit the horizon, the night air was cold. Long shadows covered most of the narrow Södermalm backstreets, leaving only the tops of the old buildings in the orange glow of the fading day. The walk out of the restaurant had been quiet, the sting of the newspaper article still lingering. I shivered, despite the heat from Niklas's body next to mine. Niklas stopped and turned to me.

"You're cold," he said softly. "You should have said something."

He pulled me in so I was facing him and slowly rubbed his hands up and down my arms.

"I still can't figure out how to dress for Stockholm weather," I said. "I thought this was supposed to be summer."

Niklas chuckled and fingered the scooped neckline of my dress. "I think you're doing just fine."

"Thank you," I said. Then I reached up to touch his face with both my hands. For a moment, all traces of the weight of the article were gone from his eyes. "Thank you for everything."

He leaned down and let his lips brush against mine, soft at first, and then, slowly, he let go of a little more of the emotion he was keeping on a tight leash. He explored my mouth with his tongue, gently biting at my bottom lip before he searched deeper. His hands slid down my back, pulling me into the muscles of his warm body. Then he broke off, leaving me breathless. He tucked my hair behind my ear with one hand and leaned close again.

"You're welcome," he whispered in my ear, just before I felt his lips on the base of my neck. I let out something that resembled a gasp or a moan, and I felt him stir against me.

He pulled away a few inches and gave a little laugh.

"We're a long way from home," he said, straightening out my dress. Then he gave me an amused smile. "Warmer?"

I nodded and laughed.

He took my hand and we continued down the empty street, up a steep hill. We turned down another street, even narrower, lined with tiny red houses and paved in cobblestone.

"Wait," I panted, stopping at the base of yet another hill. "I need to rest."

I leaned against the entrance to a dark, stone building, trying to catch my breath.

"Where are we going?" My voice came out breathless.

"There's a place up on the cliffs that looks out over the water. They have couches and heaters and blankets... and desserts. It's worth the walk. I used to go there a lot before I left for the U.S. We might even be able to catch some of the sunset. We're not too far now."

"Sounds perfect. Just give me a—" I broke off and laughed. "Wait, you're not even tired. You might need to carry me up this last hill."

He raised an eyebrow at the suggestion and gave me a wicked smile. Then he took a step closer and smoothed my hair, his voice rough and husky.

"Is that an invitation?"

All the desire, the hunger I had felt on the street a few blocks before flooded back through me, even stronger now, as his fingers touched my face again. I shivered, but this time it wasn't from the cold. How quickly these feelings came on. How quickly my body could change from laughing to wanting. I had never realized how closely my emotions—laughter, joy, irritation, anger—all could connect so directly to physical need. Was it just physical need? I was at a loss to name this feeling. Standing this close to Niklas, I wanted to speed up time, to skip forward to the place where I could feel his warm skin against mine. But I also wanted to slow down time, to stretch it out infinitely, keeping us forever in this anticipation. To never leave this moment.

"We're not in a hurry," he said. He was standing so close, our bodies almost touching. "You look beautiful. I don't think I told you that yet, but I've been thinking about it all night."

"Thank you," I whispered, smiling up at him.

Niklas cupped his hand around the side of my face,

and his thumb traced my lips.

"Whatever this is between us, it's different, Caroline," he said in a soft voice. "I don't know what it is or why it feels this way, but—"

Niklas stopped and shook his head.

"I don't know what I'm trying to say," he said. "I just want to be with you. All of the time."

His kiss was a continuation where his words had left off. He covered my lips with his, kissing me with a slow sadness he didn't bother to hide. We weren't talking about my leaving, but he hadn't forgotten. He kissed my forehead and my cheeks and then found my mouth again. I lifted his shirt to warm my hands on the muscles of his stomach, and he responded with a small yelp.

"*Whoa*, you're cold."

I pulled them back, turning red. But he took my hands and gently replaced them on his skin. His muscles contracted under my fingers and then released, accommodating the temperature. He continued to kiss me, and this time I felt a growing awareness of my fingers on his bare skin. His kisses were deeper now, longer, revealing more and more of the parts of him he had tried so hard to tamp down back in the restaurant. His hand rested on the back of my head, and my nails curled into his sides as he kissed me harder. Then he released my mouth and buried his head in the slope of my neck, and his rough breaths brushing over my skin.

"We're still a long way from home," he whispered.

"If we do this much longer, it's going to be hard to stop."

"What if I don't want to stop?"

I felt him harden against me again, but he didn't pull away this time.

"Here?" he said, looking up and down the empty street. Night was approaching, but it was far from dark.

"How about right there," I said, nodding at the dark entryway next to us that led to what looked like a school. "I've never done anything like this. I want to try."

He rocked his hips against mine, and he let out a small groan.

"Are you up for it?" I asked, suddenly unsure if I was pushing this too far.

"Oh, *God*, yes," he said with a dark smile.

He took my hand and led me up the steps, into the long, narrow entry to a large stone building. Then my back was up against the wooden door, his large hands pressing into my shoulders, and the look he gave me made my heart jump. Heat poured through my body, sparks of pleasure, all for this man. When he spoke, his voice was a ragged whisper.

"I want you so badly, Caroline. I can't—this isn't going to be gentle."

I found myself nodding back up at him, afraid of the way my own voice would come out if I tried to speak right then. The conflicts throughout dinner, our uncertain future, the minutes ticking down until my plane would leave—all of these tensions begged for release in its most basic form.

I reached down and unbuttoned his jeans, eliciting another groan from him. His hand slid down, over my hips and thighs until he found the edge of my dress. Then his fingers traveled up the inside of my leg until they reached the peak, sending tiny explosions of pleasure through me. I bit into his shirt to contain the sounds that were coming from deep inside.

"Oh, you *do* want this, too, don't you," he growled as he slipped down the last of the barriers between our bodies.

He lifted me up, and I wrapped my legs around his waist. I felt him, hard, waiting against my core. With one deep thrust, he pushed inside, and I couldn't stop my cries of pleasure.

"Oh, Caroline," came his groan, echoing in my ears as he thrust again, sending another jolt of ecstasy through me. He held me tight, my back against the wooden door, his muscles taut against mine, and still I grabbed for him, wanting him closer.

"More," I gasped.

He slid into me again and again. I tilted my hips and met each stroke with hunger for him. I couldn't get enough of him, and the need for every part of him built up, stronger and stronger.

"I'm gonna come," he groaned, and then he cried out in a long, guttural wail. He thrust one more time, and it was enough. Waves of pleasure ripped through me, and I clenched, holding onto his big body, losing myself in him. In us.

I slipped from his arms as he reached with one hand on the door to steady himself. Resting on his other arm, my legs crumbled beneath me.

"*Du är min*, Caroline." His breath was hot on my skin. "*Min*."

*

"You were right," I said, turning to Niklas. I took the last bite of the chocolate cake and then set the plate back down on the low table.

"I'm sure I was, but what are you talking about?"

I rolled my eyes. "This place was worth the walk."

"Did I say that?" he asked, looking amused.

"Yes, when I was halfway up the hill, panting. Right before—"

I stopped, heat creeping up my neck, but he just laughed.

"That's why I don't remember."

I sank back into the couch, into his arm that stretched out behind me, and Niklas pulled the blanket around both our bodies. In front of us, the water leading out to the Baltic Sea sparkled black. The sun had disappeared behind the city, but the sky still glowed a deep blue.

"I want you to stay," Niklas whispered in my ear.

The knot in my stomach tightened. I thought it was gone, but now it twisted even worse than before.

"Niklas, I—"

"Wait," he said, cutting me off before I could go on. "I don't want you to answer. I'm not even asking you to stay. You've already made your decision. I just wanted you to know how I feel."

I turned and found his lips, warm and tender. He kissed me softly and then drew back a little, smiling.

"Even that first day, when I watched you break into your apartment, I knew you were different," he whispered.

"You mean the time you slammed the door in my face?" I said with a snort.

Niklas shook his head and laughed.

"What can I say? I'm a charmer," he said with a wink. "My teammates had taken me out all night and, well, I wasn't at my best."

"But you were," I said, my voice serious now. "I never thanked you for that night. For earlier, with that guy in the park, your teammate, I guess."

Niklas nodded slowly.

"You're welcome," he said. "You know how you can repay me?"

I shook my head.

"By promising not to go out alone at night again on this trip," he said. "Or any time, for that matter."

He was studying my face carefully for my reaction. He was serious.

"Okay," I said softly. "You're right."

We were both quiet for a long time. I closed my eyes, just enjoying Niklas's body against mine.

"Maybe Tommy and Annika will decide to never come back from Brazil," I said.

"A *storybook* ending," he said in his deadpan joke voice.

I blinked at him. "I don't get it."

"Tommy and Annika? *Storybook?*" he stared at me and then chuckled. "No, I guess you don't know. Tommy and Annika are one of the most famous pair of names in Sweden, and this couple just happens to have these names. They're Pippi Longstocking's friends. The names are basic Swedish culture, along with IKEA and Volvo. The real Tommy and Annika that own your apartment must endure a lot of laughs over it. You know who Pippi Longstocking is, right?"

"Maybe," I said. At least I thought I did. He had now explained why people laughed when I mentioned their names together, but it didn't seem that funny. Was this what it was like to live in a foreign country? Always feeling one step behind, all the jokes and comments not quite making sense? But when I glanced back at Niklas, the look on his face made me smile.

"It's like if a couple were named Orville and Wilbur," he said, laughing. "You know who the Wright brothers were, right?"

I swatted at him.

"Give me a little credit," I said squeezing his muscular thigh. Now my aim was better, and he let out a little yelp, much to my satisfaction. Then he wrapped his arms around me, and I lay back in his arms.

There was a part of me that wanted to stay. Badly. I wanted to spend evenings like this, together, talking and kissing, my body against his. I wanted to explore Stockholm. Explore *us*. I didn't think I'd ever get tired of exploring us.

*

Niklas stepped out of the cab and onto the sidewalk, then turned back to help me out. The street was dark and quiet in front of our building, and he drew me in for a soft kiss.

"Thank you for the meal, the romantic dessert spot, and…" I blushed. "… and everything in between."

Niklas laughed and pulled me closer, my body flush with his.

"Thank you for a wonderful night," he whispered, "in every way possible."

He let his hand settle on the curve of my hips as we turned toward our building. But as we started forward, I could see someone standing in our entranceway. And I could already feel the knot in my stomach contract before he fully came into focus.

"Ludvig? What are you doing here?"

"The meeting went late. And I thought you'd want your contract."

How long had he been waiting there, outside my apartment? And what exactly was he waiting for?

Ludvig's eyes were no longer on me. Instead, he was staring at Niklas, taking in his arm gently wrapped around my waist. Whatever it was that he had expected, this was certainly not it. Ludvig's face reddened, and his lips were drawn into a thin line.

"This?" he spat, gesturing at Niklas. "This was more important than the planning meeting? We're leaving for Spain in a couple days, and you're out..."

Ludvig's words faded away. Niklas's arm was no longer around me. His body was no longer touching mine.

"Ludvig. *Ludvig Sundin*," said Niklas, though he was speaking to me. "Now I get it."

Niklas nodded slowly, looking up at Ludvig and then back at me. His face was hard and angry, and he spoke in a low growl that only I could hear. "You knew. Back in the restaurant, you knew he had written the article. And you didn't say anything."

An icy lump was forming in the pit of my stomach, and it was quickly spreading through me. I opened my mouth to answer but my thoughts were moving in slow motion, as if I were stuck in a bad dream.

"What did you want me to say?" I finally choked out.

"How about telling me that this was the guy who you were going to Spain with," he said, his voice still dangerously low. "Although now I think I understand why you didn't. You know what he wants from you."

He was right. But I hadn't meant to keep it from him, either, not exactly. I just hoped that I somehow wouldn't have to face this. Now, as I saw the betrayal on Niklas's face, I could also see my decision for what it was: a sacrifice of his feelings—and his trust—for the possibility of protecting myself from the mess that I had created and was now facing, head-on.

Niklas turned away from me. He passed by Ludvig without even looking in his direction and disappeared through the front door of the building, letting it slam behind him. My gaze stayed on the empty doorway, stunned by how quickly the evening had changed course. If I followed Niklas in, would I find him waiting for me at the top of the stairs, or would he close himself to me for the night…or more? Was our relationship so fragile, so close to coming apart? And, yet, something deep inside me wanted, still wanted, to give up all my other chances, all my other desires for more nights like this one. And I had hurt him.

Ludvig's voice startled me out of the downward spiral of thoughts, and for once, I was thankful.

"Should we go in?"

The thankfulness I felt immediately disappeared. Ludvig's voice was steady, as if the memory of Niklas's presence had simply disappeared. I was angry, though I wasn't sure if it was Ludvig I should be angry at. Still, I couldn't hold it back.

"No, Ludvig," I said slowly. "No, we shouldn't go in. This is clearly not a good time."

"What do you mean?" he said, his voice taking an authoritative tone. "We're leaving for Spain. Doesn't that mean anything to you? *You need this.*"

His last words dug into me. This was how he'd try

to convince me? I felt the weight of his leverage—and understood this was his intent. If he hadn't before, he had earned my frustration now.

"No, Ludvig," I said with more steadiness than I felt, "I don't need it. And I'm not going to Spain."

Those were the words I should have said to him before, and the relief at having finally said them was physical. How could I have promised otherwise?

His face contorted with anger once again, and I briefly wondered how often this change happened. His façade was more carefully cultivated than Niklas's, but there was something that felt more unpredictable about Ludvig now. Beyond his hints of romantic interest in me, I was pretty sure he was really only thinking about himself.

"How can you back out of this?" he said through clenched teeth. "You made a commitment. We can't find someone else this late."

The more he pushed me, the more I was sure I had made the right decision. I took a deep breath.

"I'm sorry I'm letting you down, and I appreciate everything you've done to help me since I came to Stockholm. As for finding a replacement, it's only been a few days since you asked me to come. I assume your team had a plan before that."

Ludvig was quiet for a moment, and then he asked, "What do you see in him?"

He waited for me to answer, but when I didn't, he said, "I get that he's rich and he has a brute appeal, the way he likes to throw around his strength, but I didn't think you were someone who could fall for that. How long will that last? He'll never care about anything but his own success. That's how they all are."

Though I had heard these lines before, they still affected me. I stood, paralyzed on the sidewalk, listening to the angry hiss of his tirade. And though nothing about the Niklas I knew matched the person Ludvig was describing, his words still grated on all the warmth and closeness of Niklas and my evening.

Ludvig seemed to sense that he had struck a nerve, and he took a step toward me.

"He doesn't care about your career, about what makes you happy," he said, quieter now. "You can never be more than a fan who strokes his ego, and one day he'll grow tired of that, even if you don't."

His last comments cut even deeper than the ones before. This man who barely knew me was spinning the worst possible version of my life. But if even Ludvig could see these problems, didn't that imply a hint of truth? Maybe, but I wasn't sure anymore.

I closed my eyes and swallowed back the tears that were threatening to spill over. When I opened them again, Ludvig was even closer. Then he took my hand and held it.

"He doesn't deserve you," said Ludvig softly.

I frowned at him. "I'm not something that a man does or doesn't deserve."

I pulled my hand out of his and walked over to the

door of my building. The cold, still air of the stone hallway hit me as I walked through the darkness, not bothering to turn on the lights. Slowly, I lifted my feet up the stairs until I came to my floor. Our floor. I stopped in the middle of the hallway, just outside Niklas's door. I listened for a long time. Finally, I heard something from deep inside, a muffled sound, low. I waited for more. Nothing. Then, through the staircase window, I saw a distant flash of lightening, followed by a low rumble of thunder. It must have been thunder that I had heard. Niklas wasn't coming to find me after the scene on the street, and I certainly wasn't going after him.

I unlocked my door and slipped into the dark apartment. Only after the door had closed behind me did tears threaten to fall. What a beautiful night it had been...until Ludvig showed up. But I couldn't blame him, not really. I leaned against the wall, replaying each of the scenes that had led to this moment, right here. Damn, I had messed this up.

I was ready for this night to be over, but Ludvig's words still wouldn't leave me alone. *He doesn't care about your career. You can never be more than a fan who strokes his ego.*

I walked into the kitchen and opened up my laptop. The next flight to Brindisi was Sunday at 6:30 am. This was my flight. Early in the morning, so the standby seat I needed would certainly be available. The trip to Spain was off now. I had turned in my second and last article from Sweden. The apartment would be gone tomorrow. I was fairly certain that my pass into the hockey games had disappeared when I said goodbye to Ludvig. All the practical pieces that had made my life in Stockholm work for the last weeks had suddenly disappeared. There was no more putting off my trip, wondering what would happen if I stayed around. The pieces I was juggling had all crashed around me, and the only one left was my magazine job. And I couldn't stay in Stockholm just to chase a famous hockey player.

But he was more than that now. I had hoped that this would somehow all work itself out, that I could somehow have Niklas and everything I wanted for myself, too. But in my rush to grab at everything, I hadn't truly thought about how these decisions would affect anyone else. And I had hurt Niklas along the way.

I took out my pen and slowly wrote the flight details on a piece of paper. Then I closed my computer and stared out the window, waiting for the same physical relief that I had felt outside with Ludvig, the relief the right decision would bring. The feeling didn't come. Another bolt of lightning flashed through the kitchen window, this one closer, and the sharp clap of thunder rattled the dishes in the cupboards. With the storm clouds moving in, darkness was settling, but I was far from sleep.

19
Packed…and ready to go?

"Tomorrow?" said Veronica, eyes wide. "But you can't go yet. You can stay with Filip and me."

We were sitting, for the last time, across from each other in Tommy and Annika's kitchen, each holding a cup of coffee.

"I have to leave now, while I still can."

"Forget Niklas. Let's think about me," said Veronica with mock exasperation. "What if I'm not ready for you to go?"

Veronica's straight face only lasted for a second, and then her smile was so warm that I couldn't help but smile back. I scooted my chair over next to Veronica's and put my arm around my friend. But when I released her, I saw a rare glimpse of sadness in my friend's eyes. I felt it too. Veronica was still my best friend, despite the fact that we had gone without seeing each other for years after college. All those years I had missed her, though I hadn't quite realized how much until I came to

Stockholm.

"I'm just worried I'll do something stupid if I stay around any longer," I said, staring down at the steaming cup in front of me.

"Like throw yourself at an incredibly hot, wealthy guy who is clearly into you?" said Veronica with a wicked smile. "I can imagine worse mistakes."

"I don't know if he's rich," I said, considering the idea. "I don't think all professional athletes are overflowing with money."

"Come on," chuckled Veronica. "He bought an apartment here in *Vasastan*, one of the most beautiful areas of Stockholm, just because he would be playing here this summer. He's certainly comfortable."

"Okay, maybe," I said and then gave Veronica a little smile. "You've certainly changed your tune about Niklas. It wasn't so long ago that you were warning me to stay away from him."

"These are selfish interests speaking. I want to have you around here a little longer," said Veronica, laughing. Then she added, "And I saw you two leaving last night. You looked... I've never seen you look at anyone like that before."

I closed my eyes and let flashes of the night before run through me: the way Niklas watched me across the restaurant table, the feeling of his arms gathering me closer against the cold evening air, his body, hot and urgent against mine in the school entryway. And the sudden absence of his hand on my hips as Ludvig spoke to me.

"Then you clearly didn't see us come home," I said, frowning.

"What happened? You had nothing to talk about when you're that far from the bedroom?"

I took a playful swipe at my friend.

"No, nothing like that," I said. "Being together with him was wonderful, complicated but wonderful, up until the end."

I gave Veronica a few highlights of the evening: the woman with the phone number, the dinner, the article, the view of the sunset, though leaving out the details from the walk, all the way up to Ludvig's appearance.

"He wrote an article saying Niklas is a liability to the Swedish national team?" said Veronica, eyes wide.

"Or any team. Like he was going after Niklas's career."

"*Dios mio*," said Veronica softly.

We both sat quietly for a long time. Finally, Veronica sighed and took a sip of her coffee.

"What you and Niklas need is some time together with no one else around. A week on a deserted island in the archipelago, to let the *magic of love* do its work." Veronica drew out those last words, exaggerating her Mexican accent enough to make us both dissolve in laughter again.

"That's actually what Niklas suggested, though not quite in those words," I said when I finally recovered. "And believe me, there's nothing I want more right now than a few more days with him, preferably naked."

Veronica smiled. "Can't you just fly down to Italy, do a couple quick interviews and then come back up?"

I shook my head.

"Not if I don't have a lot more money. My ticket only goes east, so once I leave here, I can't get back without buying another ticket. Which I really can't afford."

I ran through all the scenarios where I stayed with Niklas, looking for one where I wasn't sacrificing my job. I came up with nothing. Wasn't this the same choice I had faced with Brad just a couple months ago? But this time, the temptation to stay came in a package that was almost irresistible. Niklas was certainly no Brad.

My smile had faded. "Believe me, I've been over this in my mind a hundred times. What comes next? It'll get harder and harder to leave, but I have to leave sometime unless I'm willing to give up all my plans. And as someone wisely told me, I shouldn't feel like I'm abandoning a piece of myself."

Veronica studied me for a moment. "But aren't you abandoning a piece of yourself by leaving Niklas?"

Veronica's statement sank in, and I knew it was true, a truth I had tried hard to avoid. Either way, staying or leaving, I was giving up something big. I had been telling myself that I hadn't known Niklas for very long, that this raw desire for him would fade as quickly as it had come on, but now I wasn't so sure.

Tears welled up, and I swallowed hard to keep them in. Finally, I said, "Well, what am I supposed to do with that?"

"Oh, *Carolita*," said Veronica, putting her arms around my shoulders, squeezing me tightly. "You can always come back after your trip, right? I'll still be here."

I hugged my friend back.

"Thanks for everything," I whispered. Then I jumped up. "Wait here. I almost forgot something."

I ran to the bedroom and grabbed a flat, rectangular package wrapped in heavy brown paper. I walked back into the kitchen and placed it in front of Veronica.

"As a thank you for the interview," I said. "The piece went over really well, and it started a lot of traffic towards the site."

Veronica pulled off the paper and lifted the frame out. I had taken the photo in the coffee shop during the second half of our interview. Veronica was looking to the side, her infectious laugh lighting up her face. Against the blurry backdrop of blond heads, her jet-black hair sparkled in the sun. She looked beautiful.

"I hope you like it," I added, blushing.

Veronica nodded, her eyes sparkling. "I love it. You know I haven't laughed this often in years," she said, looking at her photo. "But you're right. You shouldn't give up your trip, either."

"Maybe I'll figure it all out in…" I looked at the clock. "…the next twelve hours or so. Who knows?"

She bit her lip and stood up.

"I have to go. I was supposed to meet Filip at his business dinner 10 minutes ago," she said. "Are you sure you'll be okay? If I'd known you were leaving today, I would have canceled."

Veronica gave me one last hug and then wrapped her photo back up.

"I know it's selfish, but I don't want you to leave," she said as we made our way back down the hallway. "Please come back. You can stay with us, or I'll find you another place to stay."

I nodded and kissed my friend on the cheek as she opened the door.

But instead of swinging open, the door came to a stop, and there was a grunt from behind it.

"Niklas," I said, peeking out. He was holding the foot that I had apparently just crashed into when I opened the door.

Veronica gave my hand one last squeeze before she slipped out and disappeared down the stairs.

"I was trying to decide if I should knock," said Niklas, a tinge of red coloring his cheeks.

"Clearly you should have," I said, gesturing at his foot.

He snorted and gave a reluctant smile.

"I'm so sorry, Niklas," I said, the words tumbling out. "I should have told you as soon as I realized it was Ludvig. I wasn't really trying to hide anything. We just have so little time, and I didn't want anything else to ruin it. Apparently, I keep making the same mistake again and again."

He leaned against my door frame so that he was now only inches away from me.

"You're stealing my apology," he said softly. "I wanted the night to just be us, no more complications. But when I saw that little shit and put everything together, I had to leave before I did something really stupid."

He brushed a stray lock of hair off my face and gently placed his hand on the base of my neck.

"And I do understand that covering the football championships in Spain is a career opportunity you can't pass up," he said. Then with a dry smile he added, "Or at least, I'm trying to understand that."

I shook my head.

"I'm not going," I said. "I told Ludvig last night."

Niklas raised his eyebrows. "So you're staying?" His eyes were filled with hope, and it cut into me.

I shook my head again and then opened my mouth to speak.

"Wait," he said gently.

Then he lowered his mouth to mine, pressing his soft, warm lips against me. I slipped my arms around his waist and hung on, pulling him closer. There was hunger that lurked behind his slow kiss, his reminder, *I am yours if you will have me*, and it echoed through my body.

"I just wanted to do that before you tell me again

that you're leaving," he whispered.

I nodded, not yet ready to speak. I found his hand and led him inside, closing the door behind us. We walked slowly down the hall, my fingers settled in his warm hand.

"Packing?" he said, glancing into the bedroom at the single suitcase next to my bed.

"Packed," I said and then turned to face him. "I'm leaving tomorrow. The flight to Brindisi leaves at 6:30 am."

Niklas's jaw clenched. He swallowed once, twice, but didn't let go of my hand. I reached up to touch his cheek. His hair was still damp from the shower, and his skin was warm and smooth. His lips met mine in another long, slow kiss, pressing me back against the door frame.

"If I don't leave now, I'll never go," I said softly, breaking off the kiss.

"Then don't," he whispered in my ear. "Stay here. With me."

The feeling was almost too powerful to resist.

"Oh, God, Niklas, I want so much to say yes. I just met you a few weeks ago, and I'm ready to give up the dream job I've waited so long for just to be near you. Just for the chance that something might work. That's what worries me."

Niklas's blue eyes were heavy on me, and I tried not to look away.

"A few weeks is enough time to decide if you want

something," he said. His voice was soft and even. "And I want you. That's not going to change."

My whole body sagged under this simple declaration. I wasn't quite sure what I had expected. That he would get angry? That he would walk out? But however I had thought the discussion would go, it wasn't like this. And I had no idea how to put into words the two opposing wants that were tearing at me from the inside. I closed my eyes and tried anyways.

"Niklas, I started on this trip because I was tired of making choices for all the wrong reasons. I've dreamed about this kind of adventure for as long as I can remember. I wanted to go far away for college, but my parents weren't ready for me to leave. And then Veronica and I planned to travel after college, but I canceled my plans to be with a guy who wanted something different. Now that I've finally gotten myself back on track, you come along, and the temptation to stay is a thousand times more powerful than it ever was before, even though I'm only just getting to know you," I said, now staring up at him. "It's tearing me up. Do you understand? It doesn't mean that I can't come back to Stockholm, but I can't give this up just because I'm falling—"

I stopped and looked down. Niklas pulled my head into his chest and smoothed my hair over the back of my head and down my shoulders. I felt dizzy, but he held me there, listening to the thump of his heart in his chest, until my breath matched his own, slow draws.

Then he cupped my face in his hands and kissed me gently.

"I'm trying to understand," he said, his forehead to mine, "I won't ask you to stay anymore. But I can't promise I won't use other methods to convince you."

I caught a glimpse of a mischievous smile before he bent down to catch my earlobe in his mouth. I sighed as his lips moved down my neck, and I could feel his smile on my skin.

"I can't believe I wasted last night thinking about you leaving instead of doing this," he said into my ear.

"Will you spend my last night in Stockholm with me?" I asked as my hands tangled into his hair.

He straightened up and gave me a skeptical smile. "Does that mean we have to go out tonight?"

I laughed and shook my head.

"Your way tonight," I said.

He raised an eyebrow, and when he spoke, his voice had turned low and husky.

"My way?"

I nodded.

"Be careful what you promise me," he said and lifted me before I could respond. Moments later, I was lying on my bed with Niklas's arms wrapped tightly around me, his body skimming over mine. Just for the sake of experiment I tried to move but was surprised at how easily he held me in place under him. He groaned in satisfaction at my attempts to move. One hand reached under my shirt and caressed my breast.

"My way, huh?"

*

"I'm going to miss this place," I said as I took the last glass Niklas had washed and dried it. I placed the glass in the cupboard and then shut the door.

"You've never met Tommy and Annika?" Niklas asked.

"No, but I feel like I know them from these pictures," I said, gesturing to the photo wall behind the table. "I think I'd rather keep it that way. Sometimes ideas are better than reality."

Niklas looked at me and shook his head. "But most aren't. Reality is messier, but it can be much better because it's something you can share, not just your own."

I wasn't sure how to respond to this. His voice was gentle, but this comment felt deliberately pointed. He wasn't going to let me go easily.

Instead of answering, I surveyed the room for any stray belongings. The only thing left of mine in the room was my laptop, sitting open on the kitchen table, in the exact same spot where it was the last time Niklas came over. He was staring at it, too.

The photo of him and the woman was still clear in my mind, and yet I hadn't looked at it since the night he had come. I had wanted to ask him about it but still hadn't. Was I scared? Not exactly. I had put off asking him for the same reason I had put off telling him about my trip to Spain: because I didn't want reality to come crashing into the magical world I was trying to create with him. But reality was coming, only hours away, and if I didn't ask now, I might never hear Niklas's story.

I took a deep breath. "Can I ask you something?"

He crossed his arms and leaned back against the counter, staring at a point far away. He seemed to know what was coming.

"Whatever you'd like," he said after a while.

"What happened back in Detroit?" I said softly. "That photo I saw in the news. Of you and that woman."

Niklas's face tightened. Yes, he had known it was coming, but the question still seemed to hurt when I asked it.

"I told you it wasn't true," he said.

I shook my head. "I didn't read the article. But I want to know what really happened."

Niklas looked at me carefully.

"I met her after a game at a bar some of us went to. There's a lot of that," he said, keeping his eyes on me.

"Women coming home with you?" I had meant to sound light, joking, but I could hear the tint of jealousy in my voice.

"Are you sure you want to hear this?" His voice was controlled. "Because it gives me no pleasure to tell you."

I closed my eyes and nodded.

"Stephanie was her name. She came home with me a few times after the games. There's something about playing hard that makes —" He looked at me and stopped.

But he didn't have to finish his sentence. I had felt it the other night. The rough, primal urge for physical satisfaction. The memory raised the flush in my face, something Niklas couldn't have missed. But the immediate desire rubbed raw as I contemplated this a little further.

"So you invited women in after a game so you could sleep better?"

He stared at me again. "I can't blame you for not liking what you're hearing, but I'm trying to be honest with you." He gave a frustrated sigh and waited. Then he added, "But I didn't invite women back to my place. I didn't want it to be that... personal."

We were both silent. It occurred to me that he had invited me in. I wasn't sure if he had said this to make me feel better.

Finally, he said, "Do you want me to continue?"

"Yes," I said. I took a deep breath and nodded at Niklas again.

Niklas looked out the window.

"It wasn't the first time with her, but I think Stephanie could feel that whatever was between us wasn't going to turn into anything more. I never told her what I wanted or expected, but I knew she wasn't happy with the way things were going. A better man would have brought it up, but that didn't occur to me at the time, either." Niklas looked back at me, his voice betraying emotion for the first time.

"Stephanie called me up one day and told me that she needed me to come over. I made some excuse, but she said it was important, something had happened. I could hear she was upset, but I agreed to come for the worst reason possible. I was hoping this would be a good opportunity to break things off with her." He gave a humorless laugh.

"When I opened my door, I was...you saw the photo," he said quietly. "I asked her who had done that to her, and she told me it was Kevin Bauer. One of my teammates. I hadn't shown up after the game, so she went home with him instead.

"I didn't want to hear any more. There's just no way to make any of this sound good, but I didn't want to know how something like that could happen. Because the truth is that as much as I know I'd never do anything like that, I'm scared of myself sometimes."

Niklas stood next to me with his eyes closed, quiet, so long that I began to wonder if he wasn't going to continue. Then he took a deep breath and spoke again.

"I tried to get Stephanie to call the police, but she wouldn't. No police, she said. She wanted me to take care of it for her instead. She wanted me to go after Bauer. And when I told her I wouldn't, she called me a coward. Told me I was just as bad as he was."

I stood, frozen, trying not to picture this scene. And failing.

Niklas ran his hand through his hair. "Should I

have gone after him? Was that the right thing to do?"

He shook his head, the corners of his mouth turned down. "She did convince me to go to the hospital, and I stayed with her while she got her face checked out. Nothing broken, so they sent her home. But someone must have seen me there, because when we came out of the hospital, there were photographers waiting. That's what you saw."

I looked at him carefully. "Why didn't you respond to the story? Why didn't you say you had nothing to do with it?"

Even as the words came out of my mouth, I knew the answer to my question. I knew a public denial wouldn't help.

"And what would I do? Accuse Bauer? Even if I had wanted to, Stephanie wouldn't have gone along with it. I didn't say anything because it wouldn't have mattered, especially with my reputation on the ice." Niklas shook his head. "And you know what Bauer did? He thanked me. Like I had helped him out, like I had kept my mouth shut out of loyalty to him. And that felt like shit, too. Then, after a game a few months later, I saw them together again in the bar."

I closed my eyes, trying to sort out what this all meant. Niklas lived in a world where this could happen, and he didn't know what to do with it. I didn't either.

"So now you know," he said, though his words sounded more like a challenge than a statement. As if to say, *what do you think of me now?*

I laced one hand in his and held tight until his fingers wound around mine.

"Thank you for telling me," I said, looking up at him.

"The hockey and everything that goes along with it—that's part of who I am, Caroline," he said, his gaze even more intense. "And I don't know what that makes me."

I lifted his hand to my mouth and kissed it. "You're not the same as that guy," I whispered. "You're not Bauer."

Niklas pulled me into him so tightly I could barely breathe. He mumbled something in Swedish into the top of my head as he pressed me closer against him. I stayed that way for a long time, a part of him, listening to his heart race inside his chest, and him a part of me, too, until I felt him stir against me. He broke off with an amused look.

"I just told you about the worst time of my life, and still I can't stop thinking about how much I want you," he chuckled. "What are you doing to me?"

I sighed. "The same thing you're doing to me."

He met my gaze, and we stood still, our bodies touching. His smile faded, and he lifted his hand to my cheeks, caressing. His face was so serious, and mine probably was, too.

Finally, he squeezed my hand and said, "Let's go over to my place while I'm still your neighbor."

I let go of him and grabbed my laptop from the

table. I looked around the kitchen one more time, I walked down the hall, scanning each room for stray possessions. These were rooms I would never see again, rooms where I had been happy. Really happy.

I felt Niklas's hand on my shoulder, and I swallowed a lump in my throat.

"I'll get your suitcase," he said, kissing me softly on my neck.

I stood at the edge of the living room for another minute and then walked back down the long hallway. It was time to leave. The ticking of the kitchen clock echoed as I walked to the apartment entrance, counting down the minutes we had left together.

"Thank you," I said as Niklas held the front door open. After one last look, I closed the door slowly and locked it behind me. "I'm going down to drop the keys in Veronica's mail slot."

When I returned up the steps, Niklas was waiting for me. He put his arms around me again and squeezed tight. Then he took my hand, and we walked across the hall.

"How about dinner?" he said. "Thai delivery?"

"Your way, remember?" I smiled up at him.

He winked at me. "How could I forget?"

*

"Can I take a few photos of you?" I said as Niklas cleared away the last of the dishes.

His face hardened immediately.

"They don't have to be straight-on," I said quickly.

"Not even your face if you don't want that. They're just for me."

He nodded slowly and unclenched his jaw.

"Whatever you want," he said softly.

"Whatever I want?" I said, with a mischievous smile. I stood up and walked over to his chair, stopping between his legs, only inches from him.

Finally, he laughed and got up, towering over me once more.

"Yes, whatever you want," he said, catching my lips with his.

I led him into the living room, still decorated with unopened moving boxes. And the red carpet. My breath quickened at the memory of Niklas and me on that carpet. But he was distracted.

"In here?" he asked, looking around.

"Yes," I said, "by those doors."

I pointed to the long, glass doors that led out onto his courtyard balcony.

"Can you move that box over a little and sit on it?" I said.

He looked inside it and nodded.

"Books," he said with a smile. "Probably won't be crushed under my weight, but not guaranteed."

"Okay. Sit facing the doors," I said. "No, more to the side."

He wore an amused look as he turned. "You're all business. You like telling me what to do, too, don't you?"

I laughed. "Maybe. Sometimes."

He nodded, still smiling, and turned his head to face the doors again. "How's this?"

"Perfect," I said. "Now just relax and get comfortable while I go find my camera."

When I returned, he was resting his forearms on his knees, staring out the window in front of him.

"Don't move," I whispered as I removed my lens cap.

I approached him slowly, taking the shot from different distances and different angles.

"Okay," I said. "Now just do whatever is comfortable."

I walked closer, close enough so that I caught a bit of his profile from the back, with only hints of the wide muscles along his shoulders and arms. I stopped, and the camera fell around my neck.

This man was mine. Mine until tomorrow morning, when I would get on a plane and leave him. I had tried so hard not to think about this, telling myself that there would be time to think about it later, but at that moment it hit me in a quiet sob.

Niklas turned around, and I saw pain in his eyes.

"No, no," he whispered, standing up.

He gently lifted my camera from around my neck and set it on the moving box. Then he gathered me in his arms and brought me over to the couch. He held me there, against the warmth of his body, stroking my hair. He let me cry and spoke softly in words I couldn't understand. He ran his hand down my arm and along my hips and thighs until my tears stopped. Then he wrapped his arms around me again and held me into him.

And he was aroused. I felt the shift, too—the sudden and urgent need to connect with him in the most basic, most primitive way possible.

"I want you now, Niklas," I whispered.

He released me slightly to get a look at my face.

"Are you sure?" he whispered. His body was tightening underneath mine.

"Very sure."

He let me go and began to move his hands along my arms, but I shook my head.

"This time, I want to explore," I said softly.

He closed his eyes and lowered his hands. "As you wish," he whispered in my ear.

Slowly, I lifted his shirt, taking in each inch of skin I revealed, running my hands over his stomach, tasting his salty-sweet skin. His muscles responded to my touch, twisting and contracting as I discovered where the ripples of his stomach met the hard planes of his chest. He helped me lift his shirt over his head, revealing the bulging muscles of his shoulders. They were firm and hot to the touch.

"Stand up," I said, shifting off him. Then I smiled. "Please."

Niklas stood up and opened his mouth to respond, but my hands on the button of his jeans seemed to stop whatever words were coming. Instead, a torn groan escaped from his mouth. I smiled and continued my slow expedition down his body, unzipping his jeans. I knelt to remove the last of his clothing, leaving his very aroused body in front of me. I let my hand settle around his thick, hard erection, feeling its throbbing weight in my hand. I looked up, but his eyes were closed, and his jaw was clamped down hard.

Then he grabbed my shoulders. "That's enough," he growled.

I gave him a wicked smile.

"Not even close," I said, releasing him, "but you can sit down on the couch."

I yanked off my clothes and stood between his parted legs. Niklas's hands pressed into my hips, pulling me down so I straddled him. We were face to face, our bodies meeting, with the hard length of him pulsing against my belly. My body urged me to go on, to guide him deep inside me, to fill myself with him. And so I did.

At that moment, nothing else mattered. Slowly I sank onto him, my body adjusted to his impossible thickness. I met Niklas's eyes, dark and full of emotion. There was pleasure there, but there was more. His eyes held fire and sadness and something else. He must have seen something, too, because for moment, neither of us moved.

"I don't want this to end," I whispered.

I lifted my hips, and as I came back down, he thrust

hard. I cried out with pleasure. He grabbed my hips firmly and lifted me again, moving me up the entire length of him before pulling me back down onto him. This time, he let out his own low groan. I never wanted this to end, but my orgasm was building so fast that I could no longer lift myself alone. He raised me and then brought my down to meet him, over and over. Our bodies moved, slick, hungry, aching together. He gave another groan, thrusting deeper, pushing me to the edge of ecstasy.

"Oh, Niklas, please."

The words spilled out of my mouth as he pulled me back down onto him. I didn't even know what I was begging for anymore. I twisted and tasted and pulled him closer, wanting more of him, all of him, as I gave all of myself to him. There was no way back from this.

20
The last seat

Niklas lowered his forehead onto mine. His sweat was on my skin, and I breathed him in. His still body enclosed mine, and I didn't want him to move. Ever. He whispered something to me in Swedish, a language that had now begun to take on meaning. I traced his lips with my fingers.

"What do those words mean?" I asked.

"They're promises."

"Will you tell me what they are?" I whispered.

"Will you come back to me?"

His words were drops of sadness, coloring the echoes of pleasure still running through me. I closed my eyes and let them sink in. At the point of ecstasy, I had begged him for more than release, and he knew it. I had begged him for the impossible—to find a way to be together. To give me everything I wanted. Selfish, yes. Because in some ways this was worse for him: While I was choosing between two things I wanted, if I left, he ended up with nothing. I was hurting him.

I wanted to say whatever it took to make the sadness in his voice go away. And I knew what it was that I could say to make it better for him. But I couldn't do it, not a second time. At some point, I would end up right where I had started at the beginning of the trip, angry at myself for sacrificing my own career, my own wants, for a man. That wasn't the foundation of any good relationship.

"I'm sorry," he said, brushing his lips against mine. "I shouldn't have said that."

My fingers grasped at his hair, holding him close.

"Niklas, would you have told me that story about what happened in Detroit if I hadn't said I was leaving? Would you still have sat for my photographs or comforted me so thoroughly just now, if I were staying?"

Niklas lifted his head and looked carefully at me. My vision was a little blurry with tears again, but I could still see the intense blue of his eyes. He seemed to struggle with his answer.

"I don't know," he said, "But does it matter? Does it make what happens between us any less real or true?"

He didn't take his eyes off me as I took in his words. I had been struggling with this idea for days, though this was the first time I had formulated it so clearly. As the days and, now, the hours melted down to the end, everything was getting more intense. Was this simply the heat of the moment? Or did it mean Niklas and I were different, that this was worth compromising for?

But he was right. These moments were real. I just didn't know how much that should matter.

*

Steam filled the bathroom, but I wasn't ready to get out any time soon. Niklas's arms were around me as the hot water came down, pooling between our bodies. It was impossible to tell where I ended and he began.

"Do you want some sleep?" I asked.

Niklas shook his head. "I'll sleep when you leave."

I took the soap in my hand and stepped back from him. Then, slowly, I began to wash his body. I took my time with the same, aching sadness as before, wanting to remember each part of him.

"What else will you do when I leave?"

"I don't know," he said. "I don't want to think about that."

He twitched and flexed as I explored the curve of each arm, the length of each finger, the slope of his back and the scar on his knee. I watched the water bead and run down his skin as I moved lower down his stomach. I heard a low groan over the sound of the water, but he stayed still, letting me explore, this time without stopping me.

I knelt down in front of him, moving the bar of soap up one leg, then the other. Finally, I put the bar down and washed the rest of him. His thigh muscles were rigid, and when I looked up at his face, his lips were parted in unspoken words. Then I opened my mouth to take him in.

Niklas let out a low cry and grabbed the wall to hold himself up.

*

We lay somewhere between waking and sleeping, as the light of the morning crept into the bedroom. Niklas's hard chest was against my back, his arms and legs tangled with mine. Our bodies fit together.

I lifted my head slightly and looked at the clock. Twelve more minutes, and then it was time to go. I had tried to resist these glances, counting down the hours, then minutes, but as the end crept nearer, I found I couldn't stop myself.

Niklas reached up and gently guided my head back down to the pillow.

"Not yet," he whispered, pressing his cheek against mine. "Just lie here and let me forget you're leaving for a few more minutes. Remember, my way tonight."

I closed my eyes and tried as hard as I could, but the knot in my stomach wouldn't go away. Everything was a last of something. The last time his unshaven cheek would rub against mine, the last time his hand would hold the curve of my hip against him. I bit my lip to stifle the emotions that threatened to swell again. Because this was my decision. And it was what I wanted, right?

I listened to his breath and felt the slow beat of his

heart on my back, though at times it was hard to tell the difference between his and mine.

The alarm finally rang, and Niklas rolled onto his back when I reached over him to turn it off. He pulled me onto his chest and squeezed me hard. He took my face in both his hands and kissed my cheeks, my eyelids, my forehead, my mouth. He stroked my hair and held me tightly, and I buried face in his neck, unable to pull myself away.

*

Across the empty street was Vasaparken, unchanged in the last month, despite the complete upheaval of my life. Not so long ago, I had imagined a mystical world with only Niklas and me. Now I was willingly leaving it.

I stepped into the taxi cab, filled with the stale cold of morning air. I looked up one more time into the windows above, but all I saw was the reflection of the gray sky. I swallowed hard and slammed the door shut.

My plan was to take the airport shuttle bus, but Niklas had insisted on the cab. It wasn't safe to take the bus that early, he argued, and leaving by cab from this side of town meant an extra hour together. I didn't want to tell him the reason I had chosen the bus: A cab cost double the bus ride or more, and without many clear opportunities to make money in the near future, I was on a tight budget. But he had insisted.

"Okay," I finally said, and he made the online reservation before I could change my mind. And when that last hour came, I was glad for it. One more hour together with Niklas was worth much more than the taxi fare.

The ride was long. The office buildings and shopping centers changed to forest, then to suburban houses, then back again to shopping centers as we headed to Arlanda airport. Thick gray clouds threatened rain but somehow brightened the green in the pastures and fields. I would miss this quiet beauty of Stockholm.

My taxi turned off the highway and finally delivered me in front of the airport. I handed my credit card to the driver, but he waved me off.

"Paid when you made the reservation, remember?"

I managed to nod as my eyes filled up. Niklas had paid for my cab. He must have known why I had resisted.

The airport was empty when I arrived, too early for the morning rush. Only one agent stood behind the long row of desks. I walked across the enormous room, the wheels of my luggage echoing in the silence of the hall. The man looked up.

"Are there still standby seats on the 6:30 flight to Brindisi?" I showed the agent my ticket.

"Not many of these kinds of tickets come through here," he said, smiling. He spoke with a perfect British accent. "Looks like a lot of fun."

I tried to smile. The agent typed something into his computer and then looked up.

"There's one seat left in economy class, but I'm

sure you'll be fine. Not many last minute purchases on early morning flights like these," he said, "but I can't issue the boarding pass until two hours before the flight departs. You can wait over there."

He pointed to an alcove along the window.

Slowly, I walked over to the sleek, black benches lined up next to the entrance way, the wheels of my suitcase echoing through the hall again. What would happen if the flight filled up? Should I take it as a sign that I should stay? The thought was tempting. I could go back to Niklas's apartment and curl up into his bed, against the warmth of his body.

But maybe Niklas would see my return in another light: When my first choice didn't work out, I came back, dragging out the goodbyes one more time until the next flight. No, I decided, I couldn't go back. Besides, the agent was right. No one booked 6:30 am flights to Italy at the last minute. Reality was much more mundane. Soon, I would pick up the ticket from the counter and say goodbye to Sweden.

I leaned back on the bench and looked at the clock. Forty-five minutes. In forty-five minutes, the last seat would be released and the rest of my life would begin. I tried to conjure up the pictures of the southern Italian farms and hills that I had poured over so many times, but the excitement I had felt even up to last week was gone.

With a sigh, I instead unzipped my handbag and dug out my camera bag. I pulled out the camera and turned it on. Then I began to scroll through the photos I had taken the night before. Niklas. I followed the expanse of his shoulders. His blond hair was messy, and in one photo, he was running his hand through it. I scrolled further, taking in each image, as if replaying a movie in slow motion, until the last one. I had caught him just as he was turning around to me, just as I had started to cry. I zoomed in. His eyes looked right at the camera, questioning me, his whole face lined with worry.

This time, I didn't try to hold back my tears. There was no one around. I just let them fall as I stared at the image on my tiny camera screen.

I wasn't sure how long I had been sitting there, looking at the photo, but gradually I became aware that other people had begun to trickle in. The airport was coming to life. I looked up at the clock. 4:25 am. In five minutes, I would pick up my boarding pass and walk through security, over to my gate.

I turned off my camera and stuffed it back into my bag. Then, slowly, I stood up and crossed the departures hall once more. When I came to the front of the line, the agent looked up at me, and his face fell.

"I'm sorry," he said. "I was wrong. That last economy seat sold. It almost never happens, but it did this time."

The nauseous combination of sleeplessness and my uneasy decision took over. I was stuck. Everything felt numb. I must have shown my distress because the agent's eyes widened.

"Let me just check the next flight… no, nothing…" He kept typing for another minute. Then he said in a gentle voice, "You have two options. You can either come back tomorrow morning and try again. There are six seats still available on that flight. Or you can pay an extra four hundred Euros to buy an upgrade for one of the first-class tickets. There are a few of those left."

Four hundred Euros. Four hundred Euros meant eight nights in the little *pensione* I had wanted to stay in. Four hundred Euros was twenty evening-long meals while watching the sun set over the water. I didn't have that kind of money to spend. But I couldn't go back and stay another night in Stockholm, either. Even if it didn't push Niklas over the edge, it would certainly wring the last of my heart dry.

"Let me think about it for a moment," I whispered and stepped aside to let the next customer by. My mind was blank.

Someone standing close behind me.

"You can go—" I started to say. But as I turned around, I stopped mid-sentence, my mouth hanging wide open.

"*Niklas*," I finally managed to say. My voice came out hoarse and scratchy, and the tears that had ebbed on the bench flowed back out. "I'm a mess," I muttered.

He was standing close to me in jeans and a dark t-shirt, with a baseball cap pulled low over his face. He took off his sunglasses, and his eyes shone into mine.

"There are no more seats left," I blurted out. "I can't get on the plane."

He brushed a stray lock of hair off my face and then put his hand on my shoulder, gently caressing me.

"There are still tickets," he said quietly. "He just told you that."

"First class," I said, shaking my head. "I can't afford that."

He bent down and whispered in my ear, "*I* can."

For the first time I noticed the duffel bag in his other hand. I looked up at him, back down at the bag and then up into his eyes again, trying to register what was happening.

"I want to go with you. If you'll let me," he said with a hint of a smile.

I opened my mouth, but nothing came out. Was this really happening?

When I didn't answer, he continued a little faster, "You can spend your days alone if you want. I won't get in your way. I just want to be with you—"

I shook my head, and my voice came back. "No, Niklas, I don't want to spend my days alone," I said. "I want to spend them with you. God, I want that."

I put my hands along the sides of his face, running my fingertips along the stubble of his cheeks as if to make sure this was real. Then I brought his face down to mine for a long kiss. I pulled him into me, closing the last inches of space between our bodies, pressing myself into the warmth of his embrace. He groaned a little.

"Careful," he chuckled when I released him. "The hotel is a long way away."

I straightened myself back up and looked around. The other people in line were staring at us. Some of them were grinning.

"Niklas," I said softly, "I can't just let you buy me a plane ticket."

I brushed my hair out of my face, trying to pull myself back together.

"Why not?"

"Because I just can't. Because—" I paused, trying to get my thoughts in order.

"Caroline, there's nothing I'd rather spend my money on," he said. "Please let me do this. We can discuss it more if you want to later, but right now let's get ourselves onto this plane before the first-class tickets run out, too."

He squeezed my hand and smiled at me.

"I just want to be with you," he said, looking carefully into my eyes. "Please can I buy this ticket so we can go to Italy together?"

Everything in me wanted this, and I couldn't bring myself to protest anymore. I couldn't do that to myself, and I couldn't do that to him, either.

"Okay," I said. "I mean, thank you."

He let his lips brush against mine once more, and then he took my hand and stepped up to the ticketing counter. The agent looked at Niklas's passport, then at him, and then back at his passport, the spark of recognition in his eyes. And I watched as the hockey player Niklas Almquist appeared, the man I had first seen at the press conference, good-humored, talkative, and in control. And I saw what he was doing. He kept his voice low, engaging the agent in Swedish, and deflecting the attention from me.

The agent handed over two boarding passes and grabbed my bag, and then, suddenly we were free. We were going to Italy *together*. Niklas's hand found mine, and he squeezed it. Slowly, we walked towards security as I tried to sort out the course of events that had changed so quickly, leaving a chaotic tumble of thoughts running through my mind. I drew in a deep breath, but it didn't take the shakiness out of my voice.

"You know, I'm going to want to eat out. At restaurants," I said.

He stopped and put his arms around me.

"This is your trip, your way," he said. Then he grinned. "Besides, no one in Italy cares about hockey."

"And I don't even know where I'm staying yet or what I'm doing," I said, my words coming faster now. "None of this trip is planned. I was just going to wait and see what happened."

He nodded and ran his hand over my hair. The warmth took my shoulders down a couple notches. "That works for me," he said softly.

"It's the middle of tourist season," I continued, "and many of the hotels will be full by now. We'll probably have to hunt for a place to stay for a while."

His hand continued to follow the path of my hair, along my face, over my shoulders and down my back.

"I don't mind," he said evenly, "though if you're worried, we can always stay in the *pensione* I booked for the next few nights."

"You already have a place to stay?"

"In case you decided you wanted to go alone," he said. Then he added, "You can still decide that, you know."

"Why would you think I would want to go alone?"

"You didn't ask me to come with you," he said gently. "I just showed up. I had to consider that you might not want me there."

I stared up at him, my mouth open.

"I didn't think to ask you, but not because I didn't want you to come," I said finally. "I just didn't think—"

I stopped. There wasn't any way to make this sound good.

He waited and then, when I still didn't speak, he said, "You didn't think a bad-tempered hockey player like me would follow the woman he was falling in love with?"

I closed my eyes, my heart pounding at his words. This was almost too much to register.

"Something like that," I said. "But not the bad-tempered part. Replace that with 'incredibly hot.'"

Niklas chuckled and bent down for a long, soft kiss.

"Did it occur to you that I might be asking the same thing? Could this incredible, sexy woman want some brute like me crashing in on her adventure?" He looked at me carefully, searching for signs of doubt. His face was serious now, and I was close enough to feel his heart pounding as hard as mine was. "You can tell me if you don't want me there, you know."

At last, it hit me: he was just as nervous as I was. Niklas had stated so simply that he wanted me the night before, and I didn't stay. Still, he came for me. I shook my head decidedly.

"No. I mean, yes," I said, flustered. I swallowed. "What I mean is that I do want you there. I really, really do. There's nothing that I want more on this trip. Or anywhere, for that matter."

He nodded, and the corners of his mouth tugged up into a small smile. I glanced down at the duffel bag in his hand, small enough for carry-on, and then looked back up into his eyes.

"But you hardly have anything with you," I said.

"Would it be too much if I told you that you're all I need on this trip?" he said with a mischievous smile.

"I don't know," I said. "Give it a try."

Niklas's face was serious now, and when he spoke, his voice was filled with real emotion. "Caroline, all I need on this trip is you."

Slowly, I slid my hand up his arm and then down his chest. This time, reality was truly better than the best fantasy I could come up with.

"No," I whispered, "It wasn't too much."

"Good," he said, with a laugh. "Besides, you didn't give me much time to pack. And I wasted most of my packing time trying to decide whether or not to go through with this crazy plan. I didn't think I'd make this flight, and then I would have been stuck trying to hunt you down in Italy."

I laughed, too.

"Okay, but what I meant was how long are you planning to stay?" I asked. "Don't you have to be back in a few days for... something?"

He shook his head and smiled. "Nope. We lost to Switzerland, so we're out of the tournament, remember?"

"Right," I said, swallowing, "but what happens after Italy?"

"I'm willing to do whatever you want," he said softly.

"You'll get bored."

He moved his hands around my waist and pulled me closer again.

"I doubt that," he said in a low voice that made me blush. Then he smiled. "And you still haven't shown me how my camera works. I figure you can teach me a little about photography, if you're willing."

"But sometime you'll have to leave me. Sometime you'll have to get back to your life, and then what happens?"

"Oh, Caroline," he said, hugging me into his chest

tight enough to take my breath away. "Yes, it's true. I can't follow you forever. Practice starts in September, and games start a while after that. But we'll figure it out when we get there."

He released me a little and kissed the top of my head.

"You're the same woman who is flying to Italy without a place to stay, without any plans further than the plane ride. You're doing this because you trust it will work out, one way or another, right?"

I nodded slowly. Niklas cupped my chin and raised my head so my eyes met his.

"Can't we trust that we'll work this out, too? I'm willing to take that gamble if there's a chance we'll be together."

He gave me another soft, lingering kiss. "I was willing to risk rejection in front of the whole Stockholm airport. And I'm ready to risk whatever else I need to be with you."

His deep blue eyes held mine, and I couldn't look away. He was offering me more than I had dared to hope for. I bit my lip and took a deep breath.

"I want this to work out so badly," I said in a shaky voice. "But it feels too good to be true."

"You might not feel that way after a few weeks with me," he said with a wry smile. "I'm not always the easiest person to be around, remember? And with all those Italian men staring at you on the beach…"

I buried my head into his chest and laughed, letting

the warmth of his body fill me again. He lifted my mouth to his and brushed his lips against mine one more time. Then he took my hand.

"Are we ready now?" he asked.

"Yes," I said, and this time I really meant it.

***

Don't miss the part two of Niklas and Caroline's story in Stockholm Diaries, Caroline 2

ABOUT THE AUTHOR

Award-winning author of sensual, emotional adventures of the heart, Rebecca Hunter is a reader, traveler, former English teacher, chocolate lover, and keeper of a very messy desk.

Over the years, she has called many places home, including Michigan, where she grew up, New York City, San Francisco, and, of course, Stockholm, Sweden. After their most recent move from Sweden back to the San Francisco Bay Area, she and her husband assured each other they'd never move again. Well, probably not.

Her debut book, *Stockholm Diaries, Caroline*, won the 2016 National Excellence in Romance Fiction Award (NERFA), and *Best Laid Plans*, her first book for the Harlequin DARE line, won the 2019 NERFA and the 2019 HOLT Medallion contests and earned a starred review from Library Journal. *Pure Satisfaction* won the VIVIAN Award in 2021.

www.rebeccahunterwriter.com